SADDLETRAMP

There came to the valley a tall, wide-shouldered man, riding a big Appaloosa stud. Trouble dogged John Cord, however much he tried to avoid it. This time he smelt death and vowed only to stay until his wound had healed. Colonel Travers had tried to warn him, had told him to ride away before it was too late. Now the terrible truth about Cord came to light, the truth that could destroy him and everything he loved. Only his blazing gun could save him.

Books by John Brand
in the Linford Western Library:

LOBO APACHE

JOHN BRAND

SADDLETRAMP

Complete and Unabridged

LINFORD
Leicester

First published in Great Britain in 1997 by
Robert Hale Limited
London

First Linford Edition
published 2002
by arrangement with
Robert Hale Limited
London

British Library CIP Data

Brand, John
  Saddletramp.—Large print ed.—
  Linford western library
  1. Western stories
  2. Large type books
  I. Title
  823.9′14 [F]

  ISBN 0–7089–9819–4

Published by
F. A. Thorpe (Publishing)
Anstey, Leicestershire

Set by Words & Graphics Ltd.
Anstey, Leicestershire
Printed and bound in Great Britain by
T. J. International Ltd., Padstow, Cornwall

This book is printed on acid-free paper

For Phyllis

Storms may be raging around us,
As through life's hectic turmoil we
   wend;
But there's always a rainbow before
   us,
When we pass through those storms
   with a friend.

1

The lone rider atop the big Appaloosa left the shelter of the tall timber, for the first time aware of the snow falling thickly about him. He frowned. It looked like a norther was blowing up and that was bad news in anyone's language. Any man with sense would head back into the shelter of the timber and wait out that storm.

But then, any man with sense wouldn't be here in the first place. Only trouble awaited him down there in that valley. He could sense it. Trouble had its own particular scent . . . one he had long since gotten used to.

It had been a fool idea anyway. A man like him had no right to dreams. The past was dead. It should stay buried. Many years had passed since he had last seen that valley stretching before him. It had been but a short visit but it had held a place in his memory ever since, helping him through five long years walking a prison cell.

He had been just a young cow-puncher then, returning to Texas from his first trail drive. As usual, he was alone when he rode into that town at the far end of the valley. He had forgotten its name or maybe he had never known, but he had never been able to forget the girl with the beautiful eyes and ready smile when she had looked at him.

Normally, he wouldn't have attended a dance or social gathering of any kind, but it had been a long lonely ride back from the railhead, and he had not yet learned to live within himself. Anyway the saloon was almost empty so he drifted across the street, liking the sound of music and happy people.

She was the first thing he noticed when he entered the hall, and he hadn't taken his eyes off her. For the first time in his life he wished he had learned how to dance, but he doubted that he would have had nerve enough to ask her anyhow. Still the feeling of her in his arms would have been something special . . . something to treasure for the rest of his life.

Their eyes had met and he turned away quickly, afraid of the emotions that she might read there. Again he felt that strange queasy feeling in his stomach. Her smile had been something special, too . . . warm and honest, tearing into his gut like a hot knife.

He had retreated into a corner, knowing he would never find the courage to speak to her. Of course, the easiest thing to do was just leave, but he couldn't bring himself to do it. He needed to savour every second he could spend just looking at her.

He had left the next morning without even learning her name, promising himself that he would come back one day. There had been no sense in hanging about anyway. He was just a footloose cowpusher with nothing to offer, but someday . . .

Things hadn't worked out the way he had planned. A lot had happened in the years since. There was nothing in his back trail to look back on with pride. He had changed. Five years in Yuma Pen had helped change him. Yet the memory of a girl with hair the colour of chestnut and gentle blue-grey eyes had stayed with him.

Now he was back, foolishly chasing a dream that could never be. She probably didn't even remember him.

He told himself that he needed the assurance that she was well looked after. That was all he really cared about. He swore softly. Hell, he was even lying to himself now.

* * *

He patted the Appaloosa's proud neck affectionately. 'You think I'm a fool, too, don't you, Warrior? You're right. There is no going back for someone like me. I took the wrong trail a long time ago.

4

'All I got down there is a memory and a lot of trouble. That's the only thing I'm sure of. All I can do is bring her pain, and that's the last thing I want.'

There was no going back. He knew that now. Memories should be buried in the past and remain there for ever. He rolled a cigarette and set fire to it, his granite face still thoughtful. Talking aloud, even to a horse, had helped. Most horsemen talked to their mounts anyway. He had needed to speak his thoughts aloud.

His face tightened. There had been enough trouble in his life already. There was no room for any more.

His mind clear, he patted Warrior again. 'Hear tell there's a lot of good country up in Canada, feller. It could mean a fresh start. Think we'll like it up there?'

He turned the horse back towards the shelter of the tall timber, his mind set. The timber would be a good place to sit out the storm before heading north for Canada.

The sudden burst of gunfire startled him and he wheeled Warrior quickly, his ears searching to locate the direction of the sound. The shot had seemed to come from down in the valley. Carefully he eased Warrior down the steep slope, every sense alert. The snow was getting heavier now, the norther building up on him.

Now, above the rising wind he could hear the sound of war cries, but that didn't make sense. This was Cheyenne country, and the Cheyenne had been peaceful for a few years now.

Occasionally a few of the young braves went on the rampage after a bellyful of cheap booze to try and relive the glory days, but that usually amounted to nothing more than a show of strength with little harm done. Maybe this was one of these times. Still . . .

For a second, he hesitated, telling himself that whatever was happening down there was none of his business

6

before he felt the Winchester slide easily into his hands, and he found himself heeling the Appaloosa towards the sound of gunfire.

The snow whipped against his face as he topped the small rise. The man below was alone against five Cheyenne braves, his rifle empty at his side as he used his pistol. Three bodies bore testimony to the lone man's shooting, but they were closing in on him now. He would be dead before he had a chance to reload.

The rider's rifle swung up in a snapshot as the Indians closed in on the man below. It was good enough. A riderless horse swept past the man on the ground. His rifle cracked again, and another Indian fell.

Even before the stranger's arrival, the Cheyenne had been losing their taste for the fight. The toll of three dead braves for the scalp of one white man was too high a price to pay.

With another gun joining the fray, the Indians lost all taste for the battle, disappearing quickly into the snow-storm.

The stranger dismounted quickly, knowing Warrior wouldn't stray from his side, despite disliking the scent of fresh blood.

Old eyes looked up at him sadly. 'Sure wish you had arrived a few minutes earlier, son. They got me good.'

He coughed, feeling the life ebb away from him. 'There is something you can do for me, son. I work for the Triangle brand a few miles from here. My wife is buried down there. I'd like to be near her. A man should be buried near someone he loves. She was the only worthwhile thing in my life. Find yourself a good woman, son, and hold on to her for all you're worth.'

That isn't much, the tall man thought wryly.

'I'm not too scared about dying, son. Thought about it a lot in the past few years. Think I'll find Maggie out there waiting for me?'

'I'm sure of it, old-timer,' the tall

man said gently.

The old man smiled weakly. 'Thanks, son. I needed that.'

He coughed again, his face screwing up with pain. 'There's a norther coming in, you won't make it to the ranch without help. My horse will lead you there. Sam is always ready to fit his nose into a feedbag, and he knows just where to find it.'

He died with the smile fading on his tired face.

The tall man lifted the old man gently, his face sombre as he tied the body across the saddle. Too bad. The old man had seemed to be someone he would have liked to have known better, given the chance. He shook his head, and swore softly. That was a damn fool thing to think. It was far easier to bury strangers than friends.

Anyhow, there was no room in his life for friends. He was a loner, born and bred that way. No involvement. Only himself to answer to.

The sudden pain in his left thigh

reminded him of the golden rule . . . always check the dead. He whirled, jacking a shell into the chamber of his Winchester in one easy motion. There was no time to aim. The Indian was on his knee, notching another arrow into his bow when the heavy slug took part of his face away.

There were no mistakes this time.

He glanced down at the arrow sticking out of his thigh, wondering if he should break off the shaft, but decided against it. It was best left to the attention of a doctor for the moment . . . if he could make it to the town.

Painfully, he climbed back aboard Warrior. There was no choice now. He had to ride into that valley, and already he could feel the tension building up in him.

There were no doubts now. Fate, destiny, call it what you would, but something had brought him to the valley . . . and trouble.

2

Col Travers had lost track of the number of times he had stepped out on to the porch. His face urgent, he tried vainly to penetrate the driving snow again. It was no use. There was nothing to see. In this kind of weather a man could be within a few yards and still not be seen. It was like being lost in a huge white cloud out there.

But Pete was out there, and he should have been back a long time ago.

Something had happened to him, that cold empty feeling in his gut told him so, and there wasn't a damn thing he could do about it. Searching for Pete would be futile, and would probably result in the loss of other men.

As foreman, that was a chance he wasn't prepared to take. Anyhow these days the Triangle didn't employ enough men to mount a search.

11

He kept looking at the blizzard, hoping. A norther was just one of the many dangers a cowpuncher faced, but Pete was too good and too old a hand to go out that way. He would have seen the signs a long time ago and headed for home.

Still the bad feeling persisted. Pete had been a part of the ranch before Travers even. If anything had happened to him . . .

Something moved in the storm. Travers cut off his thoughts quickly, hardly daring to breathe. A horse. Sam . . . Pete's horse came towards him, head down. The cold empty feeling was back in his stomach as he realized that Pete's body was tied, face down, across the saddle. There was no mistaking that old body, but how . . . ?

Another horse moved out of the storm now, a big Appaloosa stud ridden by a tall, wide-shouldered man.

Travers moved quickly then, coming off the porch to grab at Sam's reins. There was no need. The horse wasn't going anywhere. He was home. Travers looked sadly at Pete's body, vaguely aware that others had come from the bunkhouse, before signalling Chick Brody to lead the horse away.

But how? Why? Pete had been around too long to let himself get caught in a norther. Sure it happened. A lot of men had died that way, but Pete should have been too close to home for it to happen.

He glanced at the tall man on the Appaloosa for the answer. The man's face was in the shadow of his wide-brimmed stetson, yet there was something familiar about him . . . something he didn't like. He pushed the feeling aside. He would get a closer look at the stranger later. Right now, he needed an answer to his question.

'What happened?'

'A bunch of Cheyenne got hold of some cheap booze someplace and decided to take up the warpath again. They caught him up near the timber-line. He took a few of them with him to the happy hunting ground.'

He caught the still questioning look on Travers' face, and knew the man sought a further explanation.

'I was headed for Canada, figuring on sitting out the storm in the timber when I heard the shooting. I tried to even up the odds a little, but he was already dying when I got to him. He asked me to bring him back here . . . said he wanted to be buried near his wife.'

Despite the flatness of the statement, Travers believed him. The stranger, whoever he was, seemed to be in a hurry to get things said and move on out.

'That makes for a pretty thin story, mister,' a new voice said. 'Kind of hard for a stranger to find his way here in the middle of a norther.'

The stranger turned his attention to the youth standing in the doorway of the house. He knew the type; always on the prod, always ready to prove themselves. There were a lot about

. . . all hungry for a reputation.

'His horse knew the way home, boy. All I had to do was follow along behind.'

'We haven't had any trouble with Indians for a long time, mister. Funny how it started up again just when you ride into the valley.'

Soft lamplight glinted in Jane Corey's rich chestnut hair as she crossed the room towards the doorway and the sound of Brad's angry voice. Brad was always angry these days, always on the prod. Every spare moment was spent practising with his gun ready for the time when he met up with the man who had killed his father.

The tall man on the big Appaloosa stud caught her attention as she stepped out on to the porch. Her lovely eyes questioned Col Travers. There was trouble in the air, she could sense it.

Travers hesitated. There was no easy way to tell Jane the truth. Pete had been riding for the Triangle brand before he was born. He steeled himself.

15

'Pete's dead, Jane,' he said gently. 'He got jumped by a bunch of drunken Cheyenne. He was already dying when the stranger got to him.'

'We still only got his word for that,' Brad grunted. 'I didn't see any arrows sticking out of Pete.'

'Some of them were using rifles, boy,' the stranger answered quietly. 'I guess they were the ones who got Pete.'

He avoided looking at the woman. Even though he couldn't see her face, he knew her. That familiar queasy feeling in his stomach told him that she was his reason for being here; maybe the reason for his whole being.

He swore softly. Damn! This was something he had hoped to avoid.

'You carry a rifle, mister. How do we know you didn't put those slugs into Pete? It's easy to put the fault on a bunch of Indians when there are no witnesses.'

'It would have been easier for me to ride away, boy, but I gave that old man my word. And I always keep my word.'

'There could be another reason. Maybe Jud Lonegan wanted you among us. You could do a lot of damage. With us out of the way, Lonegan could own the whole valley.'

'That's enough, Brad,' Jane Corey said sharply. 'I'd like to apologize for my son, mister . . . ? I'm afraid Brad needs a firmer hand than I have been able to provide. Please try to excuse him. We're grateful to you for bringing Pete home to us.

'Please, we were just about to have dinner. We would like you to join us?'

'Sorry, ma'am, but I've got some business to attend to in town . . . if you could just point me in the right direction?'

'You won't make it, not in this weather. You could pass within fifty yards of the town and not know it's there. It would be best if you stayed here until the storm blows itself out. Whatever business you have there will wait until it's safe for you to travel.'

'In a hurry to report to Lonegan, are

you?' Brad snapped. 'What kind of wages is he paying a long-shooter these days?'

'I won't ask what you mean by that, boy, because if you gave me the wrong answer, I'd have to kill you,' the stranger said softly.

Col Travers felt the blood chill in his veins. He knew the stranger now, and Brad was in danger. A long, long time had passed since he had last heard that cold voice, but there was no mistaking it now.

Death was staring Brad in the face and the kid was too damned young and stupid to realize it.

'That's big talk for a man who isn't wearing a gun, mister. How you going to do that?'

The knife thudding into the porch post inches from his head gave him the answer. He hadn't even seen the stranger's hand move, and had no idea where the knife came from.

His hand dipped quickly towards the pistol, but Travers caught his hand,

18

putting himself between Brad and the stranger.

'You asked the question, Brad, and you got the answer. Leave it at that.'

'Damn it. He could have killed me.'

'Exactly. Remember that in future when you are thinking about opening that big mouth of yours.'

Brad was silent for a moment. The knife a few inches from his throat had unnerved him. The stranger, whoever he was, could use a knife and probably had another close to hand.

The stranger still sat his horse, his right side closest to the people on the porch. For the moment he had forgotten the arrow in his left thigh as he watched Brad. That kid was just about dumb enough to make his play, even with Travers' restraining hand.

Satisfied that the situation was under control, he turned his attention to the young girl moving out on to the porch. By her size, he guessed her to be about ten years old.

The boy was mouthing off again,

about his mother taking in every no-good saddletramp and drifter that came along. The boy was beginning to get on his nerves. It was long past time someone slapped some sense into him.

'And I'm still not buying what he said about the Cheyenne attacking Pete,' Brad snarled.

'I think you'd best keep it shut, Brad,' Travers warned. 'You don't know what you are getting yourself into, so don't push it.'

'Keep out of it, Travers. Nobody tells me what to do.'

'I do,' his mother said sternly. 'If you want to keep on living here.'

Her words stopped him. She meant what she said. His mother was a strong-willed woman; had to be to run this ranch virtually single-handed since his father had been killed.

Someday he would even that score, too.

Debbie Corey sidled up to the man on the big horse, fascinated by the Appaloosa, but stopping in horror as she spotted the shaft sticking out from the man's leg. The man was hurt, but her mother would help him. Her mother was always ready to help others.

She rushed back to her, tugging frantically at her skirts until she caught her attention. 'The man's hurt, Mommy,' she whispered urgently.

Jane Corey looked down at her daughter. The child wasn't given to lies or flights of fancy. If Debbie said something, it was so. She lowered her head to catch the child's whisper.

'What do you mean, darling?'

'The man's hurt, Mommy. There's an arrow in his leg.'

Jane looked again at the stranger, still feeling that she had seen him before somewhere, a long time ago.

'Does that urgent business in town have anything to do with a doctor?' she asked quietly.

'It might,' he admitted.

'Then I think you had better come inside. Col and I have had a lot of experience with wounds. You have a better chance with us than you have of finding your way to town in this kind of weather. Pinewood isn't a very big town, anyway.'

'I say we let him take his chances out there,' Brad snapped. 'Maybe Pete managed to get him first.'

'With a bow and arrow?' Jane asked quietly. 'Tend to his horse, Brad. Then get a couple of men to help you with Pete. We'll bury him as soon as we can get a preacher out from town.'

Reluctantly, the youth reached for the reins of the Appaloosa as the stranger dismounted.

'I take care of my own horse, boy,' the tall man said softly.

'He'll be fine with him, mister,' Travers assured him. 'Brad's got a big mouth and a short fuse, but he knows how to handle horses. He learned that from me.'

Satisfied, the stranger handed over the reins. If Travers had taught the boy anything about horses, Warrior was in good hands.

Brad looked at the arrow in the man's leg as he limped towards the ranch house, regretting his words. Travers was right; he did have a short fuse and a big mouth.

There had been a Cheyenne attack, and the tall man hadn't been afraid to face it. And he had made Brad look like a damned fool. He still didn't know where that knife had come from. He glanced back. The man was on the porch now, and the knife had disappeared.

Still there was something about the stranger that didn't sit right with him. It was no accident that he was here. There had to be a reason, but he didn't know what it was. Maybe the stranger didn't know either. There was something dangerous about the man. Col Travers had tried to warn him about it, but he had been too mad to listen.

Only one thing was sure, Travers knew more than he was telling.

3

The heat from the big fire reached out for him as soon as he entered the house. It felt good after the freezing cold outside. He couldn't recall the last time he had been inside a house. There was a feeling about it like no other. Love, maybe?

There was something more here, too. For the first time in his life he felt comfortable in someone else's home . . . almost as if he belonged here. The thought disturbed him.

He didn't belong here, or anywhere else . . . never had. Most of his life had been spent drifting from one place to another, searching for something he could never find. Himself, perhaps?

Within a few days, a week at the outside, he would be back aboard Warrior and heading north. There was

24

no place around here for a man like him.

He watched her hurry around making preparations for the job in hand, and suddenly remembered his wide-brimmed stetson, snatching it swiftly from his head, as he watched her.

She had changed, matured like wine, and even lovelier than he remembered. There was a lot of character in that face now, adding to the wonder he saw. He felt his gut tighten when she looked at him, and turned away quickly. For an instant, he was that shy young cowboy again. Already he was regretting the lost years.

Travers looked up from his examination of the arrow, aware of the tall man watching Jane's every move.

'It's gonna hurt some, getting it out. It's in pretty deep, Mr . . . ?'

He let the question hang in the air, wondering what the answer would be. It would be interesting to find out.

The stranger met his gaze evenly.

'Cord. John Cord.'

Travers shrugged. One name was as good as the next, he supposed.

Brad paused in the doorway, recoiling in horror as he saw the switch-blade knife appear again, as if by magic, in the stranger's hand. He watched the stranger hand the thin-bladed knife to Travers. There was no doubt in his mind now that if he had pushed much harder out there tonight he would be lying next to Pete, probably with that knife sticking out of his chest.

Damn it! Would he ever learn to listen to wiser heads than his own? Col had tried to warn him that he was getting out of his depth and, as usual, he hadn't listened.

The man was tough; there was no doubting that now. The sight of Col Travers digging the arrow out of the stranger's leg — he hadn't been in time to hear the man's name — had turned his stomach, but the stranger had barely winced.

John Cord liked the touch of Jane's

warm, soft hands as she cleansed and bandaged his wound. All the pain had been worth it, just to feel the touch of those gentle hands. Hell, he would have endured a lot more pain.

The little girl, spared the grim sight of Travers digging the arrowhead out of Cord's leg, returned to the room, smiling shyly at him. He was surprised to find himself grinning back at her. Showing pleasure had never come easy to him, but he found himself liking the kid. His grin reassured the girl and she came closer.

'Does your leg hurt much?' she asked.

'Quite a bit,' he admitted. 'But it will pass.'

'I always cry when I'm hurt,' she said, sounding ashamed of the fact.

'Everyone cries, honey,' he said gently. 'It's just that some people have to do their crying inside.'

'If we are going to be friends, I'll have to know your name, won't I? My name's Debbie.'

'I'm Johnny,' he answered, feeling himself getting embarrassed. He wasn't used to children, and didn't know how to handle them, but the kid had taken an instant liking to him. The thought gave him a warm feeling inside. Like it or not, he had found a friend.

She moved closer. 'I like your horse, too. What's his name?'

He told her and she smiled. 'I've got a horse, too. His name's Pinto. Perhaps we could go riding together when your leg is better?'

The kid was taking it for granted that he was staying around, but she was wrong. The first chance he had he would head out again. She had her mother's direct way of looking at someone, and that disturbed him. He avoided her gaze.

'I'll be moving on as soon as I'm able, honey,' he answered gently. 'But I'll always remember that you asked me.'

She looked disappointed. In the past few years the ranch had become a very lonely place for her. It seemed that no one had the time to spend with her any longer. Even Travers. Despite the fact that he had watched her grow up, he had never really understood children.

But Debbie had the feeling that Johnny was different, that she could talk to him and he would listen. That was important, having someone to listen to her and share her feelings.

'That's enough talk for now, Debbie,' Jane said gently. 'Mr Cord needs some food and rest. You can help me set up a bed for him in the spare room. It is warmer for you here than in the bunkhouse, and we'll be close to hand should you need us.'

He wasn't about to argue with that. The closer he was to her, the better he liked it.

The food tasted good, but fighting the storm and the loss of blood had sapped his strength. He felt weak and tired; something she was quick to notice.

'I think you had better get some rest now, Mr Cord.'

She led him towards a small, comfortable room at the far end of the main room, and left him there.

★ ★ ★

The room was quiet now as he awakened to a lull in the storm. Barely an hour had passed since he had closed his eyes. He was restless and knew only total exhaustion would send him to sleep again. His leg ached, but he ignored it as best he could, as he limped back into the main room.

He made his way towards the fire, adding fresh fuel. Only the glow of that fire lit up the room as he settled himself into an old rocking chair and rolled a cigarette.

The chill had vanished from his bones, but his leg was aching again, would for a long time yet, he reckoned. The wind was rising, howling as the norther built up to its peak. Unlike most men in cow country, he liked snow, liked the new beauty it brought to the country. Yet he could understand others' fear of the stuff. A norther was every cowpuncher and rancher's nightmare. Ranches had been wiped out overnight, the range littered with dead stock after a storm had blown itself out. It wasn't likely to happen here. The cows would head for the tall timber and wait out the storm there. Cows had more sense than most punchers gave them credit for.

He poured coffee, sipping it slowly as he heard the door open and watched Col Travers walk in, closing the door firmly behind him.

'There enough in that pot for another cup?' he asked.

John Cord nodded, knowing that Travers wasn't here just to make a social call. The man had something on his mind, and was choosing his time to get it said. He waited, watching Col settle himself in a chair facing Cord.

'I figured you'd be awake. A man

31

doesn't get much sleep with a wound like that.'

He reached into his pocket for his tobacco pouch and filled his pipe.

'Remember me, Cord?'

'I remember,' John Cord said quietly. 'I owe you for that.'

'You can pay me back by getting away from here as fast as you can. We've got us enough trouble around here already.'

'What kind of trouble?'

'The kind you are used to, but you don't want any part of it. And we don't want any part of you. We got us a range war building up around here, and we are going to lose unless we get some law around here. It's the old story, Cord. One man wants more than his share of everything this valley has to offer. He's already taken over most of the valley but he wants it all, and doesn't care how he gets it.'

'Jud Lonegan?'

Travers nodded. 'Jud Lonegan. Like I said, we got enough problems around here without you.'

'I'm not looking for trouble, Travers,' Cord said quietly. 'I'm not wearing a gun and I'll be on the trail out of here as soon as I can.'

'You don't have to go looking for trouble, Cord. It comes looking for you. I can't believe that you are here by accident. You're here for a reason. I don't know what it is, but you are in the wrong place at the wrong time. There's no future here for you, Cord.' He paused. 'All you can do around here is create a lot of heartache for everyone, including yourself. I'm not about to let Jane and Debbie get hurt anymore. They've been through enough. Try anything, and I'll stop you any way I can. Understand me, Cord?'

'I wouldn't want it any other way, Travers, but I'm not about to start anything. You've got your problems, I got mine. We'll let it go at that. I'll be out of your way soon.'

'The real problem is, Cord, none of us have any control over our destinies.

There's more to you being here than you realize.'

He let his words hang in the air as he opened the door and moved back into the night.

4

John Cord limped out on to the porch, using the makeshift crutch that Travers had provided. Three days had passed since the norther hit but the snow still lay heavy on the ground. As usual, the girl was at his side, as if afraid he would just vanish when she wasn't looking. The thought brought an amused grin to the corner of his mouth.

Travers and the others were out on the range, checking the stock.

She was talking again, but he wasn't listening, his mind elsewhere. He had barely had a moment away from the girl since his arrival, but he didn't mind. He enjoyed her company and liked talking to her, finding her amusing, and very easy to talk to. If things had been different . . . if he was a different man . . .

If. How many lives had been ruined

by that one little word?

She stayed by his side as he moved towards the stables, still talking to him as he checked Warrior and made a fuss of him. The big animal was pleased to see him, too. They had travelled a lot of miles together and come to rely on each other.

He grabbed the girl as she started to circle the stallion. 'You are too close, Debbie. You never take chances with horses. They can kill you by accident. And you never get that close to a strange horse.'

'But Warrior wouldn't hurt me,' she protested.

'I doubt it, too, but accidents happen. Don't take chances. I wouldn't want anything to happen to you,' he ended with a smile.

'I'll remember,' she said, happy now that he was no longer angry with her. She returned his smile as Cord took his rifle from the saddle sheath and started to clean it carefully. There had been no other chance since his brush with the Cheyenne.

'When are we going riding?' she asked suddenly. 'I've got a horse of my very own. Would you like to see him?'

He nodded as he finished cleaning the rifle and reloaded it. The rifle would go into the house with him. Her hand caught his and he was led out towards the rear of the stables to admire a little paint gelding. It wasn't hard to do: the horse was pretty with gentle, intelligent eyes. Debbie was in safe hands when she was aboard him. There was no doubt about that.

Debbie looked pleased as he expressed his admiration for Pinto. 'He is nice, isn't he? When can we go riding?'

Cord grinned. That was one thing she wasn't about to give up on. It was almost as if riding together would cement the bond between them. Cord wouldn't leave her then, would be? He hesitated. The kid was getting involved with him. He was getting involved, too, and that didn't fit into his plans at all.

He couldn't allow it to happen.

Col Travers was right; there was only heartache waiting here.

'I'll be leaving here in a few days, Debbie,' he reminded her gently.

'But you don't have to go. You can stay and work here. We could go riding every day then. Mommy said she would hire you if you wanted to stay.'

'I'd like to stay, honey,' he answered honestly, 'but we can't always do everything we want to do. I'm going to miss you.'

'Then don't go. We need you. I heard Mommy tell Travers.'

Her words wrenched at him, but life wasn't always as simple as a child's solution to every problem. He would slip out one morning before the child was awake. A few more days . . . just a few more days.

There would be a lot of long, lonely nights on the trail after this, but there would always be a warm glow inside whenever he thought of a bright-eyed girl and her mother. That was a memory he would always carry.

The sound of horses entering the yard distracted him. Trouble. He could smell it. The old instinct was still alive and working. Quickly, he moved Debbie towards the rear of the stables, making sure she was safe under cover before climbing up into the hayloft with his rifle and a handful of extra shells. For a moment, he paused before his bedroll, but decided against it. His past lay buried in that bedroll and he wasn't about to start back on that trail now.

Jane Corey, too, heard the sound of horses entering the yard and moved out on to the porch. It was too early for Travers and the others to be returning. Besides, the riders had come from the wrong direction. Her lovely face tightened as she faced Jud Lonegan and four of his men. This was a bad time for Lonegan to appear. She was alone . . . all the men out on the range. Knowing Lonegan, he had probably planned it that way.

Jud Lonegan was a big man, running

to fat, a fact that bothered him. It was a blow to his ego that he couldn't control his body as easily as he could control his mind.

'All alone, Mrs Corey? I saw Travers and the others riding out over an hour ago. They are a long way from here by now. That's a big mistake, Mrs Corey. A good-looking woman like you should never be left unprotected. A lot of things can happen.'

'What makes you think I am unprotected, Mr Lonegan?'

'I know how many men you employ, Mrs Corey. I counted them riding out. I'm a careful man, Mrs Corey. Careful men always get what they want. Accidents can happen when a woman is left all alone.'

'What kind of accidents, Mr Lonegan?' she asked defiantly.

'Well, I'll tell you, Mrs Corey. Harvey here is a very clumsy man. He keeps on bumping into things. He paid a visit to one of your neighbours last night. He had one of his accidents there

. . . bumped into an oil lamp. Now poor old Lem Neelson hasn't got a home anymore. The same thing could happen here.'

She faced him steadily, trying to control her fear, knowing he was quite capable of carrying out his threat, without thinking twice about it. Lonegan was a vain greedy man, hungry for power. Such men were always dangerous.

'I don't take kindly to threats, Mr Lonegan.'

'How can I possibly threaten you, Mrs Corey? I'm not even here. I'm back on my ranch with a dozen witnesses to prove it.'

He glanced around casually. 'Wouldn't be much of this place left if a fire started around here. Probably take all the out-buildings with it, too. Think you could take all this cold weather out in the open?' He laughed suddenly. 'Harvey doesn't like the cold. He likes fires. Perhaps he feels the cold more than the rest of us. Are you feeling the cold, Harvey? I think you'll find it's a lot warmer inside . . . or will be by the time you come out again.'

A weasel-faced man dressed in cast-off clothing, nodded and grinned as he dismounted and stepped on to the porch, shouldering Jane aside as he moved towards the open door.

'You won't be feeling the cold where you'll be going if you take just one more step, Harvey,' a new voice said.

Jane felt relief flood through her, leaving her weak. For the moment she had forgotten John Cord, but he was here, standing tall in the hayloft, his rifle trained on Harvey.

Lonegan turned slowly, knowing he had made a mistake, wondering who the stranger was. He had it then. It had to be the man who had found Pete, but Lonegan had counted upon him moving on. Saddletramps didn't stay long in one place.

He studied the tall man for a moment. There was no doubt that the rifle was at ease in the man's hands, ready to spout death.

'You're buying into something that's none of your business, mister. Think you can take out five of us?'

'No need, Lonegan. Without you around to pay their wages they'll just ride out. Their kind ride only for money.'

There was a lot of truth in Cord's words. No doubt his first shot would take him out. Harvey, being closest to the woman, would die next. He could see the realization dawn on Harvey's face. Harvey didn't want to die, but he knew he would if he made the wrong move.

The stranger was speaking again, his voice cold and flat. 'Before you ride out, leave your guns behind.'

'The hell we will,' a big, bearded man growled.

Cord's bullet took part of his earlobe away. He swore loudly, clutching at his ear. 'You're going to pay for that, mister.'

'Then maybe I ought to kill you right now. Save myself some trouble in the future,' Cord answered slowly. 'Travers and the others will have heard that shot, Lonegan,' Cord added. 'They'll be coming back fast, primed and ready for trouble. You want to wait around for them?'

'Do like he says,' Lonegan said flatly. 'There'll be another time. Leave the guns behind.' He glared at Cord. 'We'll meet up again, mister, and it will be payback time.'

He watched his men drop their guns into the snow, before letting his own weapons fall. Perhaps he should have called, but the man in the hayloft wasn't bluffing, and he could shoot. Bearcat Riley bore testimony to that fact.

Lonegan looked again at the stranger. He was an unknown quantity, but there was something about the man that didn't sit right. 'You got a name, mister? I get a lot of pleasure out of seeing men who cross me get their names on a tombstone.'

'Cord. John Cord. People will find it

written under yours.'

Lonegan rolled the name around in his mind. It didn't mean anything to him. Cord was nothing, just another no-account drifter with nothing but a horse and saddle to his name. Yet there was something about the man that didn't ring true, something in the way the man handled a gun, as if it were second nature to him.

He dismissed the thought quickly. The man was no threat. Hell, he didn't even carry a side gun. Within a few days he would ride out of the valley and that would be the last of John Cord . . . unless Jud Lonegan got to him first.

Wheeling his horse, Lonegan rode out of the yard, taking his men with him. Cord was right. Travers and the others would have heard the shot and be riding hell-for-leather back to the Triangle right now. The instant they saw Lonegan and his men they would begin shooting. Shooting didn't fit into his plans . . . not just yet anyway.

45

★ ★ ★

Travers held the rifle ready in his hands as he rode into the yard. He hadn't liked the sound of that single gunshot. That one sound had made the blood run cold in his veins. Jane was alone at the ranch apart from the kid, and Cord. But Cord wasn't wearing a gun!

He felt the breath rush from his lungs as he spotted the pile of guns on the porch. Whoever had come calling had left unarmed, and that was good news. It could only mean that Cord hadn't been caught flat-footed after all. He should have known better — men like Cord were never caught flat-footed.

Travers hesitated for a moment before mounting the steps, letting his relief ease the tension from his body as he recognized Jane's voice. Everything was OK. He entered the house then, the rifle loose in his hands.

'What happened?' he asked harshly.

'We had a visit from Mr Lonegan and some of his men with the intention of burning the house down. Johnny here convinced them that it wasn't a good idea. I don't think he'll be coming back here in a hurry.'

He glanced at Cord. 'Thanks, Cord. I guess that makes us even.'

She looked at Travers, wondering what he was talking about. Obviously Col Travers knew something about John Cord that she didn't. There was something mysterious about Cord, a reluctance to talk about himself, as if he was hiding something. Or was it merely her imagination?

Who was John Cord? Where had he come from? Why was he here? She had the feeling that only John Cord knew the answers to all those questions, and he wasn't about to tell anyone.

5

Rain lashed the windows as John Cord waited, his face thoughtful as he stared into the fire. Coming here had been a mistake. He should have buried Pete where he had fallen and headed away from here. But it wasn't to be. Something else had taken control over his life. Fate? Destiny? He didn't know, but something was guiding him.

Any minute now Col Travers would walk through that door. There were things that needed to be said, and Travers needed to do the talking. He heard the latch open and watched Travers come in, grim-faced and tight-lipped. He stopped before Cord, heedless of the rain dripping from his slicker on to the rug.

'It's time for you to move on, Cord. We can't afford any more trouble around here. There's a little town about twenty miles north-east of here. You can make it by noon tomorrow, if you set off early before anyone else is up and about.'

'Meaning Debbie and Jane?' Cord asked.

'That kid's attracted to you, Cord, and I think her mother is beginning to feel the same way. They want you to stay around. I don't. I know how much trouble you carry around with you. You proved that today.'

'I was all they had between them and Lonegan today, Travers. You were out chasing cows, remember? It was pure blind luck that my rifle was out there in the stables.'

'It takes just one shot to start a range war, Cord. You know that as well as I do. You may have fired that shot today.'

'Lonegan isn't going to talk about today. His pride won't let him. And he won't want anyone to know that he was within ten miles of this place. If we don't talk about it, neither will he.'

'I still think you are in trouble, Cord.

And I still want you out of here.'

'I didn't want to come here, Travers, and I'm not looking for any kind of trouble. I'll make sure everything is under control before I ride away. I owe them that much. Right now, you need all the help you can get. I know Lonegan's type. You are already out-numbered three or four to one. Lonegan hires guns, and tough boys. All you got is cowhands.'

'They are all I need, Cord. I'm running a ranch. All I need are cowhands. And they are under orders not to get involved in any kind of gunplay.'

'Brad going to follow your orders, Travers?' Cord asked quietly.

'OK, so Brad's a hothead, but he still follows my orders. None of my men carry guns when they go to town. That goes for Brad, too. that's my way of avoiding trouble. You got a better way, Cord?'

'Nope . . . as long as it works. How long do you think you can keep Brad on a tight rein like that? I've seen his kind before. They are always looking to make themselves a reputation. Brad's just itching to get that first notch on his gunbutt.'

'Not around here, Cord. He's got his sights set on higher things . . . like getting the man who killed his father. I can keep him under control. Brad's got good blood in him — mostly Jane's I'd say. I'm not going to let Brad off that rein. Just one mistake, that's all it takes. You know that better than most.'

He moved towards the door, stopping with his hand resting on the latch. 'Do yourself a favour, Cord, ride out as soon as you can. There's more at stake here than you know about.'

The door closed behind him, and Cord was left alone with his thoughts again; staring into the flames as he rolled a cigarette. Travers knew something that he didn't know. But Travers didn't want to part with that information . . . not yet anyway.

'Was that Travers?'

The words startled him and he turned quickly to watch Jane move into the room dressed in a pink robe.

'He wants you to leave, doesn't he?'

'We discussed it,' he admitted slowly. She poured coffee, handing him a cup. 'What did you tell him?' she asked softly, afraid of the answer.

'I told him I would stick around until I thought it was time for me to move on again.'

The smile only half-touched her face. The thought that he might move on again bothered her. Still, a lot could happen between now and then.

'Why do you feel the need to move on?'

He shrugged. 'Who knows? Maybe it's something in the blood.'

'Perhaps you are just looking for a place to belong,' she suggested.

'Men like me don't belong anywhere. We spend our whole lives looking without even knowing what we are looking for.'

'You could find it here,' she said

quietly. 'We like having you around and Debbie adores you. Even Brad is beginning to have second thoughts about you.'

'That leaves just one member of the family to win over,' he said softly.

She smiled, that special warm smile that he loved so much. 'We all want you to stay. You came back here for a reason, Johnny. I don't know what that reason is, but I'm glad you came back.' She laughed at the puzzled look on his face. 'I have a good memory, Johnny Cord. I knew I had seen you before, the moment you entered the house. Tonight, I remembered where and when. It was a long time ago, at a Saturday night dance in town. I remember a tall young cowboy strolling into that dance. He watched me all night, but was too afraid or shy to ask me to dance. He left town next morning without me even learning his name.'

'He couldn't dance, and you were better off not knowing his name,' he answered quietly.

Her eyes searched his face, wondering what his statement meant. 'I always knew that we would meet up again some day,' she said softly.

'It was an accident,' he said curtly. 'If Pete hadn't been caught up in that fight, I'd have been halfway to Canada by now.'

'Life is full of accidents, Johnny,' she answered gently. 'But some people prefer to call it destiny.'

6

The town seemed to be just as he remembered it. A little larger maybe, but he couldn't be sure. He hadn't spent much time in the town, and every town seemed like a city to a young cowpuncher after three months on a trail drive.

He eased himself slowly to the ground, making sure his stance was steady before helping Debbie down from the driving seat of the buckboard. She had insisted upon driving him to town. Despite her youth, she knew horses and handled them well. That was probably down to Travers, too.

The fact that she had insisted upon driving him to town and spending so much time with him bothered him a lot. He loved having her with him, enjoying her idle chatter, but didn't like the fact that she was becoming too attached to him. There would be only tears when he left, and the last thing he wanted was to see her hurt.

'The doctor's office is this way,' Debbie said, taking his hand.

'He ain't in,' the old man seated on the boardwalk ouside the saloon said. 'Probably won't be back for the rest of the day. Maybe even tomorrow. Mrs Waterman lives 'bout twelve miles outside town. She's expecting her fourth. Usually takes about twelve or fourteen hours. Doc says he's never seen the like.'

He paused long enough to bite off a fresh wad of chewing tobacco. 'I just saved you a long wait, mister. Figure that's worth a drink?'

'I'm with someone,' Cord reminded him.

'It's OK, Johnny. I can go play with my friends for an hour,' she said eagerly, hoping he would agree. She wanted to see her friends, tell them all about John Cord. He was becoming everything to her. None of the other girls had a friend like him . . . someone to really talk to. No, he was more than just a friend. He was more like the father she hadn't really known. All she had was a vague memory of a man who never seemed to have much time to spend with her.

Johnny wasn't like that at all. He liked having her with him, liked having her talk to him, and showed it. It was almost as if he were the missing part of her life.

He nodded agreement and she ran away happily to join her friends. He wouldn't be long anyway. Cord wasn't a drinking man, rarely having more than a couple of beers at one sitting. The old man was grinning toothlessly as he watched Cord mount the steps slowly. He would have his drink.

'The name's Jonas. You must be Johnny Cord. I heard what you tried to do for Pete. I owe you for that. Pete was a good friend.'

Cord shrugged it aside as he followed the old man into the saloon. His leg ached, throbbing with pain from the jolting ride in the buckboard. It would be good to sit and rest his leg before facing that rough ride back to the Triangle. Debbie was a good driver, but it was impossible to avoid all the ruts in that trail back to the ranch.

He settled himself in the chair, letting Jonas get the drinks, setting them on the table before them. Jonas licked his lips as he savoured the shot-glass of rye, as Cord sipped slowly at his beer.

Cord studied the saloon. Nothing had changed here. It was just as he remembered it, almost empty, with the deeply scarred bar. He relaxed, turning his attention back to the old man. Jonas was a man who liked to talk, when he could get anyone to listen. Most people avoided Jonas, knowing they would get stung for a drink, but Pete had been a friend, always seeking him out to buy him a drink or two. He had been at Pete's funeral, and shed a few tears for a dear friend.

Cord hadn't been at the funeral but

Jonas had heard about him and how he had been hurt in trying to save Pete's life. There had been no mistaking John Cord when he had come into town with Debbie. His limp had confirmed it.

He emptied his glass quickly, looking with dismay at Cord's barely touched beer. The man wasn't a drinker. That was bad news. Jonas had hoped to get in a few more drinks before Cord pulled out.

Bearcat Riley grinned as he recognized the tall man seated at the table with Jonas. He let the batwing doors swing shut behind him, aware of the sudden hush in the saloon. He liked that. It meant people were afraid of him. He liked people to be scared of him.

He touched his still sore ear reflectively. There was no mistaking the man who had done that to him. Now it was payback time. The stranger didn't have a rifle with him this time, and there was no sign of a hand gun.

A lone crutch rested near the tall

man's chair. Good. That would make it easier. The fact that the stranger was virtually a cripple didn't bother him. Cord would learn never to butt into Jud Lonegan's business again.

His grin widened as he stopped before Cord's chair. 'Remember me, pilgrim? I remember you. I got a memento of the last time we met. Now I'm going to give you something to remember me by. On your feet, pilgrim.'

'He's got a bum leg, Bearcat,' Jonas reminded him.

'Yeah, I hear he got that by mixing into someone else's fight, too. He's gotta learn that it doesn't pay. You gonna learn that lesson, pilgrim?'

Cord started to rise to his feet slowly, trying to keep his body relaxed, ready to roll with the punches. It was the best he could do. He was in for a beating, and there was no way to avoid it. His leg wouldn't last out in any kind of fight. All he could hope for was to get in a few good licks before Riley took him out. Riley was a big man, but in Cord's experience most big men couldn't punch, relying on brute strength to beat others into submission.

The first punch caught him high on the head as he was still in the act of rising, driving him backwards over the chair. A heavy boot thudded into his bad leg as he struggled to rise again. A knee caught him in the face driving his head backwards, and again he felt a heavy boot slam into his ribs. Riley's grinning face hovered over him as he struggled to rise. The fist slammed into him again and again. Strangely, there was no pain, only anger as he slipped into unconsciousness.

It was only a brief respite. Within a few seconds he was awake again, watching Riley's grinning companions drag him back. The pain hit him then, and he feared one of his ribs had been cracked . . . maybe more.

Through the haze of pain he heard someone tell Bearcat to take it easy, Mr Lonegan didn't want anyone killed

— not yet anyway. He struggled to rise but Jonas held him down. It wasn't difficult. Right now he felt as weak as a newborn calf.

'Take it easy, Cord. I'll borrow a mattress from the hotel and we'll get you back to the ranch. Mrs Corey will take care of you until we can get the doc out to you.'

'Johnny!' the child's distraught cry hurt Cord more than Riley's fists. He wondered just how much of the brutal beating she had witnessed as she rushed towards him. He tried to grin but it hurt too much. Instead he reached up to touch the tear-stained face gently.

'I'm OK, honey. After I'm cleaned up a little you won't even know I've been in a fight.'

'You wish,' Riley laughed. 'Get out of here, little girl. You can come back in a few years' time.'

Debbie backed away from him, frightened by the brutal figure.

'Wait outside, Debbie,' Jonas told her. 'Harry, go to the hotel, get the

62

mattress. You can help me with Cord when you get back.'

Cord pushed his restraining hand aside and struggled to his feet. It would be easier for the kid if she saw that he could still walk, with a little help from Jonas.

'You'd best drive me back to the ranch, Jonas. I don't think Debbie is in a fit state to do it.'

'I was going to suggest it,' Jonas said, glaring at Bearcat. 'Kids should never see that kind of thing.'

Riley and his two companions looked pleased as they watched Cord being helped on to the mattress resting in the bed of the buckboard. Even with that soft cushion, it would be a rough ride back to the ranch, and Cord would feel every bump. More pain for the tall stranger. Riley liked that idea.

Jonas settled himself in the driving seat of the buckboard glancing over his shoulder at Debbie lying at Cord's side, holding on to him desperately as she struggled to control her tears. Riley had hurt the kid too, almost as much as he had hurt Cord. And that was one thing that John Cord would never forgive.

He looked at Riley then, letting his loathing for the big man show. 'You're a fool, Bearcat. You really think you've stopped him, don't you? He'll be back, and he'll destroy you. You'll spend the rest of your miserable life hiding from shadows. He'll be back. Think about it, Riley. I'll remind you because I'll be sitting right outside that saloon every day from morning 'til night waiting until I see John Cord ride down this street, step down from his horse and go inside. I'll be right behind him, Riley, because I want to see him tear you apart. I got the feeling that he's going to make it look very easy.'

The words disturbed Riley. There was something about Cord that bothered him. All through that beating there had been no sound or sight of pain from the tall man. Only a very tough man could take the kind of punishment that Riley had inflicted without showing pain.

'I hope you're right,' Riley blustered. 'I'll finish the job next time. I won't be hard to find.'

'You'll be looking for a place to hide after he's finished with you,' Jonas grinned, setting the horses into motion.

*   *   *

Jane had finished the laundry, and was taking the clothes out to the washing-line when she heard the buckboard approaching. She felt the panic grip her as she realized that Jonas was driving, and there was no sign of Debbie or Cord. She dropped the laundry back into the basket and rushed forward to meet the buckboard.

She felt a faint sense of relief as she spotted Debbie's head over the back of the wagon bed. She was holding on to something as her tearful face turned desperately towards her mother.

Jane rushed forward, stopping in her tracks as her eyes looked down on John Cord's battered face and body. She knew now how Debbie felt.

'Bearcat Riley,' Jonas said. 'The kid saw it.' He grinned suddenly. 'Never thought I'd see the day when I felt sorry for Bearcat Riley, but that day is coming.'

7

The tall, thin figure in the black frock-coat stepped out of Cord's room and stopped before the fire to pour coffee into a tin mug.

'How is he?' Jane asked anxiously, knowing Doc Bishop wouldn't give her an answer until he had filled his pipe and had it going to his satisfaction. A thick cloud of smoke rose from his pipe, before he finally glanced at Jane.

'No need for me to ask who did that to him. I've seen too much of Bearcat Riley's handiwork. But he made a mistake this time. I've seen men like Cord before; they are far tougher than Riley could ever hope to be.'

'Hell, he's too scared to even wear a gun,' Brad said. 'He'll never get anywhere near Riley again.'

Doc Bishop blew a cloud of smoke towards the ceiling, his face placid.

'He's got nothing to prove, boy. He knows what he is and just what he is capable of, and doesn't feel the need to prove it to anyone else. He'll be back on his feet within a week and he'll go looking for Bearcat then. May the good Lord help Riley, because I sure hope I won't be around to do it.'

He drained his coffee mug, then, looking slowly at Brad, said, 'I brought you into this world, boy. I figure that gives me the right to say something: don't cross John Cord. You are not going to live long if you don't start learning about people.'

'I ain't scared of nothing or nobody,' Brad snarled.

'That's what makes you a fool in my book, boy,' Doc Bishop said calmly as he moved towards the door. 'Take the time to think once in a while. It might make the difference between life and death.'

Silence followed his exit. Col Travers rolled a cigarette. There was no need to add anything to Doc Bishop's words. It was good advice, but he doubted that Brad would ever take it. Brad was a hothead. He had set ideas about everything. Any man who didn't carry a gun on his hip wasn't a man in Brad's book. And until the day that John Cord strapped on a gun he wouldn't be a man in Brad's eyes.

Travers hoped that day would never come.

Jane entered the darkened room quietly, looking down at the man on the bed, before turning up the lamp. Cord's eyes. were closed, but he wasn't sleeping. Somehow she knew that just as he always knew when she was near. His eyes opened, and he gazed at her with a strange calm.

'How do you feel?' she asked, knowing it was a stupid question. How could she expect him to feel after such a beating?

'Like I've been caught in a stampede, but I'll live.'

It was typical of the man that he made no threats against Bearcat Riley.

'How's Debbie taking it?'

'She finally cried herself to sleep. She thinks the world of you.'

'I'm sorry. I didn't mean for that to happen.'

'Is that such a bad thing . . . having someone to love you?'

'It is when it can only end in tears. She'll be hurt again when I ride out.'

'You don't have to ride out. You could have a future here . . . if you wanted it.'

'Men like me have a past, Jane, not a future. It's a fact of life and there's nothing anyone can do to change it.'

'You thought you had a future once, Johnny, and I was part of it. I'm the reason you came back here. We both know that.'

'I was a kid then, Jane. Kids have dreams. After a lot of long, lonely nights on a trail drive, a drover is likely to fall in love with the first female he sees. Memory of her stays with him on his next trail drive, or until he meets the next girl. The memory becomes a lie that he can't escape, even if he wants to.'

'Am I a lie, Johnny? Do you want to escape from me?'

He watched her carefully, knowing she needed the reassurance of his words. Despite the façade of toughness, Jane Corey was a vulnerable woman, needing to be told that she was still desirable. That was all any woman really needed.

Cord shrugged mentally. Hell, they were only words.

'Maybe, Jane, but not for the reason you think. You've been with me for a long time now. I guess you always will be. And you were there with me when I needed you most.'

The words brought a smile to her face. At least, he hadn't lied to her. But she wondered what he meant by her being with him when he needed her most?

John Cord was a strange man; his emotions and thoughts well hidden, allowing no one else into the inner sanctum of his mind, except perhaps Debbie. She wondered if he had ever been able to share his feelings with anyone else? It seemed that only Debbie could penetrate the armour John Cord had built around himself.

But, at least, for a brief moment, he had shared himself with her. Her smile broadened then vanished quickly as she heard Debbie cry out, and knew the child was having a nightmare . . . reliving John Cord's brutal beating.

She rushed from the room, letting the door swing shut behind her.

Cord's right hand tightened into a fist. He, too, knew what Debbie was going through, and it was all his fault. He should have stayed away from the valley. Only a fool chased a dream that could never be.

He could feel the anger rise in him; his own pain forgotten as he focused on Riley's grinning face as his fists and heavy boots thudded into Cord's body. Again he heard Debbie's anguished cries as she tried desperately to stop

Riley inflicting more pain on Cord.

That was the worst kind of pain, knowing he hadn't been able to help the child when she had needed him most.

He rolled a cigarette slowly and lit it. An old coffee lid on a low chest of drawers at his bedside served as an ashtray. The spent match dropped into it among the other dead matches and butts.

The kid was hurting and Riley had laughed at her. But Riley wouldn't be laughing for long: Riley would never laugh again. His days as a tough guy were numbered. One day soon he would see a tall man on a big Appaloosa stud ride into town, and that would be the end of Bearcat Riley.

For the first time in his life, John Cord would enjoy beating a man half to death.

8

Brad watched John Cord limping painfully across to the horse corral, enjoying the feel of the early morning sun on his face. The tall man was a big disappointment to him. For a brief while it looked as if he had found someone to stand beside him when it came to a showdown with Lonegan. Jud Lonegan was moving in on every ranch in the valley, only the Triangle standing strong against him, but it was only a matter of time. That was a fact that they had to accept.

For a while, after the incident when Lonegan had bought his men to the Triangle and Cord had stood them off, it looked as if Cord was going to make a difference. But it wasn't to be. The fight with Bearcat had proven that. He had handled Cord like a rag doll. Hell, Cord had spent the past four days in bed, and Riley didn't even have a scar to prove he had been in a fight.

Travers was wrong about John Cord. The man was a coward. The fact that he was too scared to even carry a gun proved it.

Col Travers moved out of the bunkhouse, carrying his usual cup of coffee, pausing as he noticed Brad studying John Cord. Brad was on the prod again; he knew all the signs. He had known Brad too long. The boy was foolish; too young to read men and realize just how dangerous men like John Cord could be. He could only judge a man by the speed of his gunhand.

'If you are thinking of going to town, Mr Cord, it's that way.'

Cord ignored him as he gazed around. The sun felt good on his face. It was his first glimpse of the outside world in four days and he liked what he saw. Spring was moving in quickly. Most of the snow had already disappeared, leaving only a few patches in the hollows that he could see.

As yet, there was no sign of Debbie, but that wouldn't last. Soon, she would be up and about, in her usual place at his side. He was beginning to feel incomplete without her at his side, and that disturbed him. He didn't want to break the child's heart, but it would have to be. There was no way to avoid the heartache when he saddled up and rode out. It wouldn't be easy for him, either.

'Bearcat Riley has issued a warning to every Triangle rider, Mr Cord. Any Triangle hand who rides into town from now on gets what you got. I guess he's got the idea that we are all as easy to handle as you are. He's wrong.'

'Cord was a cripple when he faced Riley, Brad,' Col reminded him.

'That just meant he couldn't run away, Trav'. Mr Cord doesn't believe in violence. Hell, he hasn't even got guts enough to carry a gun. Guns scare you, don't they, Mr Cord?'

'Only when they are in the wrong hands, boy,' Cord answered softly.

'I'm not scared of guns, Mr Cord. Bearcat Riley will find that out if he ever tries to lay his hands on me. He's not about to stop me riding into town any time I feel like it.'

'You'll follow orders, the same as anyone else, Brad,' Travers told him. 'I don't want anyone riding into town until this thing is settled one way or another.'

'That's one order Mr Cord will be glad to follow,' Brad grinned.

'Cord isn't riding for Triangle yet, Brad. He makes up his own mind about what he wants to do. I got no say in it.'

'Well, you got no worry on that score, Col,' Brad said, watching Cord return to the house.

'You're wrong about John Cord, Brad,' Travers said quietly. 'If you don't start learning how to read men pretty damn quick, a sombre-faced man will be reading words over you . . . but you won't be hearing those words. John Cord will settle with Riley when the time is right. I'll bet my saddle on that. Until that day comes, I want you and every other Triangle man right here on this ranch.'

'I'll take you up on that bet, Travers. One hundred dollars against your saddle.'

'I'll spend it in town,' Travers grinned. 'Maybe I'll even contribute towards Riley's medical bill.'

His grin broadened as he watched Brad walk back toward the bunkhouse. It was going to be the easiest hundred dollars he had ever earned. He would get a lot of satisfaction out of seeing Brad count out his winnings into his hand ... maybe even insist on being paid in dollar bills. That would really bug Brad.

The kid was a fool, too young and single-minded to realize that John Cord was unlike other men. He made his own laws and lived by them. Pride and his own ego meant nothing to John

Cord. He had nothing to prove.

In some circumstances, Cord would have ignored Riley's brutal beating, but Riley had hurt the kid, too, and that was something that Cord could not forget or forgive.

Riley would have to pay the price for hurting Debbie, and the nightmares she had suffered since. John Cord would destroy him — handle him in a way that would make him a laughing stock for the rest of his miserable life.

One day soon, John Cord would climb aboard that big Appaloosa stud of his and head for town. That day would signal the end of Riley's reign as a tough guy. Soon. It would happen very soon. The tall man was getting stronger physically and mentally every day, and already chomping at the bit to get to grips with Bearcat Riley.

Knowing John Cord, there was little doubt that he had already planned his strategy, having relived every second of his last brush with Riley. By now,

John Cord would know every one of Bearcat's moves and how to counteract them.

Travers almost felt sorry for Bearcat Riley. Brad, too, if he didn't learn to keep his mouth shut. The kid would have to learn quickly about men like John Cord if he wanted to go on living.

The only thing that had kept Brad alive so far was that he was Jane's son and Debbie's brother. But a man could only be pushed so far, even a man like John Cord.

The man was a volcano, ready to erupt. Travers could already sense the tension building up in him. Cord knew trouble was coming, and knew there was no way he could avoid it. Most men would have cut and run by now. John Cord had a lot more than most to lose, more than he even knew. But he had made his commitment and would back it to the hilt. Men like him always kept their word, even if it was an unspoken promise.

Problem was there was something

that Cord didn't know . . . something that Travers hadn't yet told him. Maybe the truth would never come out. Travers hoped not.

It would destroy John Cord.

9

A sudden thought occurred to Jane as she hung the washing on the line. The jeans that Cord had worn when he came into the valley with Pete's body, had been washed, patched, but in all honesty were not really fit to be worn again, even though he was wearing them now.

Surely he had other clothes in his bedroll, a spare pair of pants and a couple of shirts perhaps? The least she could do was wash, and perhaps mend them if needed. The bedroll was indoors on the top of the small closet. Surely he wouldn't mind if she attended to those little chores for him?

No. He wouldn't mind; he would be grateful. Johnny was always grateful for everything she did for him. And he would notice when he returned.

Debbie had finally got her wish. This

morning, Cord had saddled his horse for the first time since coming into the valley. Debbie had watched him fearfully, afraid he was going to ride out of the valley, and it would be the last time she saw him. That fear had been living with Debbie for a long time — her mother, too, if the truth were known. But it was a fear that wouldn't die. Until John Cord gave his personal assurance that he wouldn't leave, that fear would stay with them.

The trouble was Cord couldn't or wouldn't give that assurance.

The bedroll was heavier than Jane expected. For a moment she hesitated. Perhaps she shouldn't be doing this? Everything a cowboy owned was carried in a bedroll. It wasn't much. Hardly room for many personal items. Perhaps just a faded tintype or two. They could be avoided. Besides, he wouldn't mind, she told herself.

Her mind made up, she unwrapped his bedroll, stopping in horror at the sight of the big black Colt with the

mother-of-pearl grips. There was something frightening — ominous almost,
in the sight of that lethal-looking
instrument of death. She shuddered.
Somehow the thought of John Cord
with that gun strapped to his waist
disturbed her. She prayed that she
would never see him wear it.

There was something evil, eerie,
about that weapon, as if it had a life of
its own — perhaps even controlling
John Cord's life. Certainly it looked as
if he were unable to part with it.

She shivered again at the thought,
quickly rewrapping the black Colt and
gunbelt into the bedroll and placing it
back on top of the closet, grateful for
the fact that it was no longer in sight.

Perhaps she had found the reason for
Cord's reluctance to talk about himself?
For some reason John Cord had put the
gun aside. Good. That evil-looking
weapon was a part of John Cord's past
and she hoped it would remain so.

★ ★ ★

John Cord heard the gunshots as they approached the small rise. The Winchester slid quickly into his hands as he jacked a shell into the chamber. He glanced around for cover. Nothing much, just a small stand of scrub oak. It would have to do.

His main concern was for Debbie, wondering if he should send her back to the ranch. No. She would be safer at his side. At least that way he could protect her. Once she was out of his sight, there was no telling what might happen to her.

'That's Mrs Coleman's place,' Debbie said.

'OK, stay by my side. Do everything I tell you, when I tell you, and do it quickly.'

There were no further shots as he topped the small rise, and noted with relief that five riders were heading away from the small homestead, leaving a woman standing alone in the yard. At least, she didn't seem to be hurt.

Still cautious, they rode down into

the yard. The woman would recognize Debbie and not use that old buffalo gun she carried in her hands. A black and white sheepdog lay dead near an old outbuilding. Carefully, he moved Warrior between the dog and Debbie, knowing how upset she would be at the sight. If the truth were known, it upset him too.

'Tap wasn't much of a dog, mister,' the woman said quietly, barely able to hide her emotions. 'Getting old, too. Almost at the end of his time, but they had no call to shoot him. Tap did a lot of barking but he never hurt a soul in his life. I don't know the name of the man who shot him, but I'll remember his face. Next time they come calling I'll make sure of getting the first shot in.' She looked sadly at the dog. 'He was company, I'm gonna miss him.'

'If you take Debbie inside, Mrs Coleman, I'll take care of him for you.'

She nodded, as if afraid to speak for the moment.

He returned a half-hour later, to find

hot, fresh coffee and cookies waiting for him. Debbie seemed happy enough in the woman's company so he relaxed. The hard years of work had taken its toll but she was still a handsome woman.

She was studying him now with direct, still moist eyes. 'You must be John Cord. Col Travers told me about you, said you were the man to see if I ever needed help of any kind. You must be one hell of a man if Col Travers set such store by you. Before the trouble started, Col used to come visiting a lot. We used to sit out on the porch most evenings and talk.' She smiled suddenly. 'People used to do a lot of talking about Col and me, but the plain fact is Col is scared of women. Guess I'm the only one he ever felt comfortable with. I've been missing out on those little talks lately. He just stopped by one day to tell me about you. He sets a lot of store by you. But for some reason he's scared of you. I don't know why. You ain't about to hurt Travers, are you? I wouldn't like

87

it if you hurt Col Travers, Mr Cord.'

'When I get back, Mrs Coleman, all I'm going to do is offer Travers some sound advice. If he takes it, he will be spending a lot more time on that porch with you.'

He blew an easy smoke-ring, watching it drift upwards, before speaking again. 'I've got to say that Col Travers never struck me as much of a ladies' man.'

'He ain't. I guess he's scared of women, but he's kind of comfortable to have around. At least, with a man like Col you know his eyes ain't going to be wandering in any other direction. That says a lot for any man. Shame more women don't realize it. I guess you and Travers are alike that way. Trouble is, I don't know how to catch a man the way Jane does. She doesn't even know she is doing it. Guess I just ain't got the right equipment for it.'

'You've got the right equipment,' Cord said. 'And Travers knows it. Problem is you could be a mite independent for Travers' taste. Some men don't like that. They like to feel needed. It makes them feel like men.'

She pondered on his words for a few minutes. There was a lot of truth in Cord's words. Trouble was, she had been independent for too long. But maybe she would prove a good enough actress to give it a try. It was worth it.

A too independent woman was a blow to a man's pride. And it took a man like John Cord to tell her that. Damn it. She should have realized that herself. After all, she was supposed to have a woman's instincts, wasn't she? Only one thing was certain at present, Col Travers would find a different woman when next he visited her.

John Cord got to his feet slowly. His leg still hurt a little but a couple more days would settle that. Then . . . He left the thought unfinished as he stepped out on to the porch. It was time to get Debbie back to the ranch before her mother started to worry. She knew that John Cord would gladly give his life in protecting Debbie from harm, but accidents happened. And a mother's instinct was always to worry.

He helped Debbie mount Pinto before stepping aboard Warrior, looking down at Sadie Coleman as he thanked her for their welcome.

'It was a pleasure having you here, John Cord,' she said honestly. 'You gave me some good advice. Now I'm going to give you some. Get out of this valley as fast as you can.'

'You sound like Travers,' he said.

'We've talked about you,' she admitted. 'I guess he needed someone to confide in. There are some things that need to be said. He doesn't want to see you get hurt. Neither do I. You can save yourself a lot of grief by riding out now. The truth will hurt you more than any beating Bearcat Riley can hand out. And that's the kind of pain you will feel for the rest of your life.'

10

It was time. John Cord tested his leg. Good enough. A little stiffness, but that would work itself out by the time he got to town. As Cord crossed the yard to the stables, one of the hands was trying to take the kink out of a fresh bronc, watched by Brad and Travers. Neither man was aware of him.

For once Debbie wasn't at his side as he saddled Warrior and stepped into the saddle. He was aware of Travers watching him as he rode out into the early sunlight, his face tense.

'Wait for me, Johnny,' Debbie cried.

He wheeled Warrior towards Debbie and Jane waiting on the porch. The granite look that Jane had never seen before stared at them. This was a different John Cord to the one they had known. She felt a chill run through her body. Perhaps this was the real John Cord.

'Not this time, sweetheart,' he said softly.

The big stud was eager to travel. There were no further words as he heeled the big horse out of the yard.

The child looked up at her mother desperately. 'He's not leaving us, is he, mother?'

'Not yet, Debbie. He'll be back. There's something he has to attend to in town.'

Strangely she felt no fear for him. That look had told her more about the man than she had ever known before, hadn't even suspected.

★   ★   ★

Jonas strained his eyes, a grin spreading wide on his face. There was no mistaking that big Appaloosa or the man aboard him. He had been waiting a long time for this. But there had never been a doubt in his mind that John Cord would one day come riding back into town.

Today was going to be the sorriest day of Bearcat Riley's life.

His grin was still wide as he stepped into the saloon, widening even more as his eyes settled upon Bearcat Riley in his usual place at the bar. No doubt Riley had thought he would never see John Cord again, but he was wrong. Only a fool thought like that. Anyone who knew men would have known John Cord would be back.

Any minute now, Cord would come striding through the doors behind him. Jonas would enjoy the look on Riley's face when that happened. None of Riley's other visitors had ever come back for more after one of his beatings. This would be a first. Jonas wondered how Riley would react when he saw Cord come through those doors. It would be interesting to find out.

For the first time Riley seemed aware of Jonas's presence as he turned to face him. 'You won't find no free drinks in here today, old man. Most of your friends are too afraid to come into town anymore.'

'Not all of them, Bearcat,' Jonas grinned.

The wide grin puzzled Riley. There hadn't been much for the old man to smile about since Bearcat had issued his warning to all Triangle riders. 'Something funny, old man?'

'You won't think so, Bearcat,' Jonas laughed, his eyes never leaving Riley's face as he heard the batwings open behind him. The look on Riley's face told him that John Cord had just entered the saloon.

For the first time ever he saw doubt grow on Riley's face. No one had ever recovered so quickly from one of Riley's beatings. And no one had ever come back for more.

He stepped aside, looking at Cord for this first time. But this was a new John Cord from the one he had met in this saloon barely a week ago. The man who faced Riley now was cold, hard and ruthless; ready to take Riley apart. If

Riley had any sense he would start running now . . . or begging John Cord for his life.

There was an easy confidence in that relaxed body as he faced Riley. Cold, hard eyes chilled Riley's blood, but he ignored it. Hell, he had beaten Cord once before. He could do it again. Cord wouldn't have forgotten that beating yet, and that gave Riley the advantage. There would be no mistake this time, no one to pull him off. Anyone who tried would have to face the consequences later.

This time Cord would end up as a cripple for the rest of his life — or die.

'I'm back,' Cord said softly.

'That was your last mistake, pilgrim. This time I'm going to kill you. I'm going to find out just how tough you are,' Bearcat snarled.

His first punch missed by inches as Cord barely swayed to avoid the blow. The tall man had fast feet and fast hands. Riley screamed and felt sick as Cord's first punch thudded into his ribs, breaking one.

The tall man could hit and he knew where every punch was going. Another punch thudded into the already broken rib, and he screamed aloud again. A hard fist slammed into his eyebrow and he felt it split wide open. Blood flooded his face until he could barely see, but still the punches came, sapping his strength, destroying his will. He almost wished that Cord would kill him, bringing relief from the pain that flooded his whole body.

The old fool had been right after all. Cord was handling him just like a rag doll . . . destroying him easily with every punch. As yet, Cord didn't bear one mark of the conflict. The funny thing was Cord didn't seem to be enjoying the job he was doing on Bearcat Riley. It was just something that had to be done . . . a statement to be made.

Cord could take him out any time he wanted to . . . kill him even. The thought frightened Riley. He had been quite ready to kill Cord, but . . . He felt sick as the strength drained from his body. But Cord wasn't finished with him yet. He stood back, measuring his punch carefully. Riley felt the darkness claim him as the fist slammed into his jaw. It was a grateful relief from the pain as his body slid down on to the bar room floor.

* * *

Doc Bishop lit his pipe blowing a thick cloud of black smoke towards the ceiling. Business was slack, but that was good news. He could relax and perhaps catch up on his reading of the latest medical journals. He was looking forward to that when he heard the urgent knocking on the door. Oh, well. He would look forward to reading those journals some other time. Maybe there was something of interest in them.

'The door's open,' he yelled, determined not to rise from his comfortable chair if he could help it. The man entering his office he knew only by sight, not by name. It wasn't important anyway. If the man had made it this far on his own feet he wasn't an urgent case.

'You are needed at the saloon, Doc. There's been a fight.'

Doc Bishop swore silently. Riley again. Some fool cowpuncher had wandered into town, ignoring the warning, and run into Riley's fists. He could only hope that too much damage hadn't been caused, but knowing Riley that wasn't likely. The man liked to inflict a lot of pain.

He reached for his bag. 'How bad is it?'

'Pretty bad, Doc. I've seen a lot of fights, but I never seen the likes of this one before. He beat him physically and mentally. Doubt if Bearcat will ever be the same again.'

'Bearcat?'

'Sure. John Cord walked into the saloon and just took him apart. Riley never even laid a hand on him. Cord made it look easy . . . beat him to the punch every time. Made everyone wonder how they were ever scared of Bearcat.'

Doc Bishop grinned. Bearcat Riley. Old Bearcat had finally become a victim, and John Cord had been the one to take him apart. His pace quickened as they crossed the street towards the saloon. He would enjoy seeing Riley in pain.

His first thought was for John Cord as he entered the saloon, examining his hands carefully before turning his attention towards Riley with a brief glance. Cord had certainly made a mess of the big man. Too bad he had missed it.

'Mrs Johnson is expecting her second baby,' he said. 'I'll be back after the birth. He'll keep until then.'

'Mrs Johnson isn't due for another two months, Doc,' someone pointed out.

'I'll have a cup of coffee while I'm waiting,' Doc said dryly. His little joke over, he stooped to examine Riley. The man would never get involved in a fight again. That much was sure. Like the man said Cord had destroyed him both physically and mentally. He would spend the rest of his life hiding from shadows.

Hell, even a nine-year-old kid would be able to frighten Riley after this. It looked as if he would be having Riley's company for a long time until the man healed and was on his feet again.

He wasn't looking forward to that. On the other hand, every time he treated the big man for his wounds he would cause him pain. That was something he couldn't help, but the thought of it did have a certain appeal.

'Some of you carry Riley to my office. I'll be along after I buy Mr Cord a drink.'

'We're together, Doc,' Jonas reminded him.

'Make that three, Charlie,' Doc told the bartender. It was a big day, a cause for celebration. Bearcat Riley was no longer bull of the woods, never would be again. Cord had destroyed him.

★ ★ ★

The wild cry from Chick Brody as he galloped into the yard brought everyone from the buildings. Despite orders, the kid had sneaked into town to see his girl. When he saw Cord ride into town and enter the saloon, he had followed along. Hell, Cord might need help. The least he could do was cover Cord's back. The fight, if it could be called that, was something he would never forget. The ease with which Cord had handled Bearcat Riley had amazed him. There was no doubt that Riley was a tough man — he had proven it time and time again — but Cord had handled him like a baby. That was something that Brad should have seen. He would have changed his opinion of John Cord.

'The town's wide open again. Cord took Riley out of the line-up. Never seen the like. Riley never stood a chance. Doc reckons he'll spend the rest of his life running from a fight.'

He dismounted, enjoying the look of disbelief on Brad's face. 'You should have seen it, Brad. Riley never laid a hand on him. That John Cord is one hell — sorry, ma'am — of a tough man. Made it all look so easy. I sure wouldn't want to mess around with him.'

He hoped Brad was getting the message. Despite Brad's quick temper they were friends, and he wouldn't want to see anything happen to him. But if he kept on pushing Cord the way he had been . . .

Hell, any man could only expect to take so much, even Cord.

* * *

There was a satisfied look on Travers' face as Brad counted out the money into his hands. Brad still hadn't gotten used to the idea of Cord beating Bearcat Riley, but there seemed to be a new respect for the tall man growing in him. Travers wondered just how long that respect would last if the truth about John Cord were ever known. He hoped it would never come out. It would destroy a lot of lives, not least John Cord's.

11

'Looks like we finally got a man among us,' Lem Neelson said, as he paced the main room of Jane Corey's home. The meeting had been called following John Cord's destruction of Bearcat Riley. For the first time it seemed, with John Cord's help, that they had a chance to oppose and even beat Jud Lonegan at his own game.

At least there was hope now, something they had never had before. Travers was a good man, and what he said made sense. But he didn't know how to handle men like Lonegan. Neelson had the feeling that Cord did.

Up until now, they had stood no chance against Lonegan. That was something they had to accept. But Cord was different. He was a man without fear. And he could use a rifle.

He had proved that the day he had stood off Lonegan and his men the day they had decided to visit the Triangle.

One man without fear could make the difference, Neelson told himself. Travers would defend Triangle with his last breath, but he wasn't prepared to take the fight to Lonegan. That much Neelson was sure of.

Cord wouldn't settle for that. He had taken the fight to Bearcat Riley and beaten him easily. He could do the same to Lonegan. Lem Neelson wanted his ranch back, and he had the feeling that John Cord was just the man to get it for him.

The tall man was standing near the window, looking out at the driving rain, seemingly uninterested in the outcome of the meeting — if there was to be an outcome. Most meetings he had been to resolved nothing . . . just a lot of empty words. But they made men feel important.

'With Cord backing us, Lonegan will think twice about trying anything,'

Neelson said. 'If we stand together we can beat him.'

'You don't stand a snowball in hell's chance,' Cord said softly.

'Cord's right, Neelson. Start anything now and Lonegan will kill you.'

'Right now, Lonegan has got some rethinking to do. With Cord backing us we've got the edge. Lonegan won't like that.'

'Nice of you to put Cord in the front line, Lem,' Travers said. 'There's just one problem: this isn't Cord's fight. He doesn't even ride for the Triangle. What happened beween him and Riley was personal. He doesn't owe you, me, or anyone else a damned thing.'

'Besides,' Brad added. 'Mr Cord doesn't like guns. He's afraid of them. If there's any real shooting to be done that's up to us. How good are you with a gun, Neelson?'

'There'll be no shooting,' Travers said. 'That's just what Jud Lonegan wants. If we fire the first shot we'll be playing right into his hands. And we won't stand a chance then.'

'That's your idea, Travers, not mine,' Brad said. 'I can take care of myself.'

'And my job is to take care of everyone else,' Col reminded him. 'Any shooting starts, and a lot of other people are going to get killed. It's time you learned that a bullet can destroy more than one life.'

'You're starting to sound like Cord, Travers.'

'Well, that ain't a bad thing, boy. Maybe it's time you started to listen to him, too.'

'Why? Because he beat up on Bearcat Riley? That supposed to make him bull of the woods now?'

'You already lost a lot of money betting against him, boy. Didn't you learn nothing from that?'

Brad looked at John Cord. 'You got some wise words for me, Cord?'

'Travers already said most of it. It just takes one hothead to start a range war, and you won't stand one chance in hell of living through it. All you got is a lot of cowpunchers and homesteaders. Most of you don't know one end of a gun from the other. A lot of Lonegan's men are already being paid gun wages. When the shooting starts he'll be hiring professionals. You'll be up against the best.'

'I can handle it,' Brad said defiantly.

'I doubt that, boy. I doubt that very much.'

'How would you know, Cord? You've never even seen me pull a gun.'

'I don't have to. I've been around long enough to recognize a real fast gun when I see one . . . and I don't have to see him clear leather to know it. They've got a look about them that's unlike any other. I've seen kids like you, too — would-be gunfighters. Most of them get their names burned into wooden markers before they reach twenty-one. That's too high a price to pay for a reputation.'

'Maybe they weren't as good with a gun as I am,' Brad said.

'They thought so,' Cord said quietly.

'I'll prove it one day,' Brad snapped.

Cord shook his head slowly. He was starting to lose all hope for the kid. Brad had a one-track mind, centred on the gun on his hip. The gun was beginning to control Brad, instead of Brad controlling the gun. He shook his head again. There had been a lot of kids like Brad along his back trail, most of them dead and forgotten by now except by grieving parents or girlfriends.

The boy was too eager to start building a reputation, but it would prove to be a short-lived one. That much Cord was sure of. But, at least, there would be tears at Brad's graveside. Sometimes, somewhere after he left this valley, John Cord would die, but there would be no one to grieve for him.

Maybe that wouldn't be such a bad thing. At least, Jane and Debbie would be spared that much pain. The man they had once known as John Cord would die without them even being aware of it.

12

The sudden burst of gunfire startled John Cord. Without thought, the rifle slipped into his hands. Trouble? Somehow he didn't think so, but he was taking no chances. He set Warrior in an easy run towards the sound. If his guess was right, he would soon come aross Brad practising with his gun.

He shook his head slowly. Brad was a fool, and fools had to learn the hard way. It was time someone had a long talk to the boy. Travers had tried but Brad wasn't about to listen to him. What did Col Travers know about guns anyway?

It looked like it was down to him, but it was probable that Brad wouldn't listen to him either. Sure it was none of his business. If he had had any sense he would have climbed aboard Warrior and lit out of the valley as soon as he was able.

Still the picture of Jane and Debbie standing at Brad's graveside haunted him. It would end up that way. There was nothing more sure . . . unless the kid saw sense. There were too many kids like Brad about, all destined for an early grave. Brad would have to discover that he wasn't the fastest gun alive before learning the hard way.

He dismounted, still carrying the Winchester, as he soft-footed up to the rim of the gulch. His guess was right. Brad was down there, thumbing fresh loads into his pistol.

'That's two mistakes, boy,' Cord said softly. 'And one is too many.'

Brad turned quickly, glaring at Cord as the tall man came towards him. 'One, you let yourself get caught with an empty gun. Two, you let me soft-foot up on you. Either of those mistakes could prove fatal.'

Strangely, Brad didn't feel mad at Cord. The tall man was right. He had been caught flat-footed on both counts.

'Everyone makes mistakes, Cord. It happens.'

'Not when your life depends upon it, Brad.' Cord said softly. 'Any man who sets out to make his way with a gun can't afford mistakes. There is always someone ready to take his place, and a lot of them don't care how they do it. Ever stop to consider how many gunfighters have been shot in the back, Brad? The day you strap up a gun and set yourself up as a gunfighter you set yourself up as a target for every would-be gunslick in the country. You live in the shadow of the gun for the rest of your life, and that's the one thing you can never escape from. All you got to look forward to is death. Too many men have made that mistake, Brad. You are no longer a man; you become a reputation. Just a name. Everyone is waiting to see that name on a tombstone. The day you kill your first man in a gunfight, Brad, and I hope that day never comes, you will find that there is no turning back. Every rep-hungry punk will come looking for you. You'll no longer have a life of your own. Every shadow becomes a threat. You'll be afraid to turn your back on any man again . . . even a friend. Is that the kind of life you want, Brad?'

There was a new respect in Brad's eyes. He had never heard John Cord speak so much before, but he seemed to know what he was talking about. Maybe there was more to John Cord than he realized.

'For a man who doesn't carry a gun, Cord, you seem to know a lot about gunfighting.'

'I've been around, Brad. I've seen a lot of gunfighters . . . seen the way they have to live. Never known one who didn't regret the day he first strapped on a gun. Don't make the mistake they did.'

'There's still something that I have to do, Cord, and the only way to get it done is with a gun.'

'There's always another way, Brad,

but you got to be man enough to find it. The day you take another man's life you destroy your own.'

Brad finished loading his gun, and put it back into leather, his eyes never leaving John Cord. 'There is no other way, Cord. This is something that I have to do. I've been waiting too long for it . . . almost half my life. Trouble is, Cord, you don't think I'm good enough, do you? You are afraid that I'm going to get killed. But the fact is, you don't give a damn if I get killed or not, you are thinking of Ma and Debbie, how they would feel if that happened. I guess I can't really blame you for that. It's kind of nice to know that someone will be around to take care of them when I leave.'

'You are wrong about me not caring what happens to you, Brad. You are Jane's son and Debbie's brother. That makes you important to me, too. I'll do anything I can to stop you getting yourself killed.'

'You still don't believe that I'm good

enough with a gun, do you, Cord? Guess I'll have to prove it.'

His hand dipped suddenly, his Colt barking twice and the tin can he had been using for target practice leapt into the air.

'Impressed, Cord?' His eyes sought the tall man's approval.

'I've seen better,' Cord said softly. 'A lot better. Any fast gun could take you out.'

'Maybe you could do better? Why don't you show me, Cord? Want to borrow my gun?'

'I got nothing to prove, kid,' Cord said softly. 'But I'd listen to some good advice if I were you. You'll live a lot longer.'

'You sure talk a good fight, Cord, but I never knowed of anyone winning a fight with words.'

'Maybe not, kid, but they sure don't die from them either.'

'They say that Jack Bodell is the best there is. You ever come across him?'

'You could say that,' Cord answered

slowly, his face tense as he wondered where Brad was leading the conversation. Jack Bodell! That was a name he had hoped never to hear again. 'Men like Bodell are best left alone, Brad. He tends to his own business and doesn't go looking for trouble. That makes him more dangerous than most. Besides nobody's heard of Bodell for a long time. Some say he's dead. Maybe it's better that way.'

'I don't believe it, Cord. Bodell is still alive someplace. Maybe he's just lost his nerve, but he'll turn up one day and he'll find me waiting for him.'

'That's a sure way to get yourself killed, Brad. Bodell had quite a reputation . . . even the top guns steered clear of him.'

'I'll take him,' Brad said confidently.

'Bodell's no threat to you. He's best left alone.'

'I owe him, Cord. I made myself a promise a long time ago that I would be the one to kill him. That's a promise I intend keeping. I'm good enough to take him now. What do you think, Cord?'

'I think he'd kill you, Brad. He wouldn't like doing it, but after a man has been using a gun for as long as Bodell he'd have no choice in the matter. Survival becomes a matter of instinct. With a gunfighter that instinct lies in his gunhand. Bodell would kill you before he even realized that his gun was in his hand. He'd regret it, but . . . '

He let his words fade away, hoping that Brad would understand what he was talking about. He paused, not sure that he wanted the answer to his next question.

For a moment, he decided against asking that question. Jack Bodell was dead. Let him remain that way. That name had already haunted him for a long time. Too long. Men like Jack Bodell should not have existed in the first place. They were a product of their times, and would soon become extinct. That time couldn't come soon enough for John Cord.

He watched Brad replace his gun into leather, his hand lingering on the smooth walnut butt. That was one of the first symptoms: the gun was becoming a focal point of Brad's life. And that was a bad sign.

'I can take him, Cord.' He patted his gunbutt. 'This is the tool of my trade, Cord. And I can handle it better than any man alive.'

Cord rolled a smoke and set fire to it. He had heard those words before . . . damned fool words.

'Is that how you think of a gun, Brad, as a tool? You're wrong,' Cord said softly. 'It is not a tool. It's a weapon. It was designed for one purpose only — to take life. Any man who thinks of it as anything else is a fool. The day you strap on a gun, Brad, you'd better be ready to use it, and that means taking someone else's life. And every time you take a life something dies inside you, too. Soon, you'll find that there is nothing left inside you. You'll be as dead as the men you have killed.'

'There's only one man I want to kill, Cord.'

'Yeah, Jack Bodell. You got a reason for wanting him dead, Brad? Or is it just his reputation you are after?'

'I got a reason, Cord, a good one. Jack Bodell killed my father!'

13

Cord stared into the dark rainswept night, his eyes unseeing, his taut-muscled body unaware of the chill in the air. It was time to move on. Travers had tried to warn him, but he hadn't been listening. Sophie Coleman had tried too, but to no avail.

He had no choice now.

Finally he had come face to face with the truth about himself and the fact that he had no future here. There never had been a future for him here, but he had been unwilling or unable to accept that fact.

Two more days, he told himself. Two more days. At least that would give him a chance to face Jud Lonegan and maybe get him to change his mind about taking over the Triangle. It wasn't much of a hope, but he had to give it a try.

He had come to the valley, hoping to stir up some long dead ashes in the hope that a fire still burned beneath. The fire was still there. She hadn't forgotten him. Love had been born that day a long time ago and had not died. Now he had to bury those ashes again and bury them deep. But the memories would always burn bright and forever.

Cord rolled a cigarette, still unaware of the chill of the night, or the blue-green eyes watching him. Her voice startled him, and he turned quickly.

'I said, it's warmer inside, Johnny,' she repeated quietly.

He followed her inside, for the first time aware of the cold as she poured coffee into two mugs.

Those lovely eyes searched his face. 'You are leaving, aren't you, Johnny?'

'Soon,' he admitted slowly.

'We don't want you to leave, Johnny. We need you. You belong here.'

'I don't belong any place, Jane. I'm a drifter. Nothing but a no-account saddletramp. I'll never amount to anything. It's been that way all my life, and I can't change now. When a man like me gets the urge to travel he has to move on and there's no looking back. I need to be free, live my life in my own way with no one to answer to.'

'Are you running away from me, Johnny?' she asked quietly.

He shook his head slowly. 'No, Jane. That's the one thing I can't run away from, you and Debbie will always be with me. I'm running away from myself, but there's no escape from that.'

'Then don't run away, Johnny. Stop and face it. Whatever you are running from we can beat it. Together we can defeat anything. We want you — need you — here with us. It would break Debbie's heart to see you go.'

'She won't see me go, Jane. I'll disappear one morning before anyone else is up and about. It's the best way. There won't be any goodbyes because I don't have the courage for that. Just keep telling Debbie that I've gone away for a while, and pretty soon she'll forget about me. It's the best way.'

'She won't forget, Johnny. Neither of us will. And I'm not about to start lying to her. I've always told her the truth. She expects it from me. If I start lying to her now, she would never forgive me. That is something you are going to have to face up to yourself, Johnny. You are going to have to tell her goodbye, and give her your reasons for leaving — if you want to go on calling yourself a man.'

She let her words drift in the air like smoke before speaking again. 'Are you man enough to do that, John Cord? You can't give me your real reasons for leaving, but can you tell a little girl the truth? Or do you intend lying to her, too?'

'You are not making this any easier for me, Jane.'

'Should I? Is there an easy way to break a child's heart? You mean everything to her.'

'I tried not to get involved. I didn't

want anyone to get hurt by my being here.'

'But you are involved, Johnny, just as we are. And we are not the only ones who are going to be hurt by you leaving here. You are going to be hurt, too, and perhaps more deeply than any of us. You've had a glimpse of what might have been for you. Everything you have ever dreamed of lies right here. You'll spend the rest of your life looking back at what might have been. Can you live with that, John Cord? I don't think so. This is where you belong, with two people who love you very much. I don't care about your past. I only care about our future.'

Her misty-eyed loveliness upset him, and he turned away quickly. He wanted to believe her words, share his future with her, but that could never be. A man could ask for nothing more than to spend a long winter evening just looking at the wonder of her beauty.

'I'll talk to Jud Lonegan before I leave,' he said harshly. 'Maybe I can get him to see sense. No land is worth dying for.'

He heard her bedroom door close and heard her quiet sobs before he returned to his own room.

A lot of problems would have been resolved if he had died with Pete up near the timberline.

14

The four men sat in a dimly lit corner of the saloon deep in subdued conversation. Jud Lonegan was holding court, and his men were paying close attention.

The fat man sat with his back to the wall, taking no chances. He had made a lot of enemies since his arrival. The three men facing him, apart from Brazos, had been working for him ever since he had come to the valley.

As yet, Brazos was an unknown quantity, although there was little doubt that he could use the gun on his hip. But Brazos had proved to be something more than just a quick-trigger artist. He had a cool head and a quick brain that set him apart from most gunfighters.

Lonegan was angry. 'If we can break Triangle, I'll own this valley in a month,' he seethed. 'Col Travers has been a thorn in my side for long enough. If we can get rid of him we'll have Triangle at your mercy. The others will pack and leave soon after.'

'Why don't we just shoot him? Push him into a gunfight? Hell, any one of us could take Travers in a shoot-out,' Dorey Stroud said. 'It will be a pleasure.'

'You don't listen very good, do you, Stroud?' Lonegan snapped. 'When the shooting starts I want Triangle to fire the first shot. That way we get the law on our side. After that, it's open season on Travers and every other Triangle rider.'

'There's no way that anyone can push Col Travers into a gunfight,' Coby Lane said. 'But the kid is different. He's a hothead, always on the prod. Wouldn't take much to push him into a fight.'

Lonegan smiled. Coby had a good idea. It could work. It would work. All they had to do was catch Brad with a gun on his hip. Problem was Col

Travers had given orders against carrying guns in town. Somehow, Jud Lonegan doubted that Travers could hold Brad on such a tight rein for long. Brad didn't take kindly to orders and was just itching to prove his prowess.

The time would come, and Lonegan could afford to wait. Brad would be the one to light the fuse. He was sure of it.

'That just leaves John Cord,' Coby said quietly. 'We gotta figure on him, too. Have to say that I don't like the idea of going up against him. There's something about that man that doesn't sit right.'

'Then I guess he's mine,' Brazos said quietly. 'Who is he?'

'He's the one who took out Bearcat Riley with his fists. A tough man in a fight. Ask Bearcat — if he ever gets around to talking sense again.'

'I won't be swapping punches with him,' Brazos said. 'How good is he with a gun?'

Coby shrugged. 'Doesn't carry a handgun. Only seen him carry a rifle, but he can use it. That's something else Bearcat can testify to. I wouldn't be taking any chances around him, was I you, Brazos.'

Brazos grinned, unable to take offence at Coby's remark. 'I never take chances, Coby. I like living too much.'

He looked thoughtful for a moment. 'John Cord, you say? Name doesn't mean anything to me, and I know all the good ones. You can count him out. Mr Cord won't be any problem. I'll handle him.'

All four men turned their heads as the batwings opened and the tall figure of John Cord entered, his Winchester hanging loose and ready in his right hand. He paused before the four men.

'I've come to talk, Lonegan. I want you to leave the Triangle alone, settle for what you've got.'

'And if I don't?'

'Then I'll have to come back and kill you,' Cord said softly. 'I'm leaving the valley soon, but I'll be close enough to know what's happening. At the first sign of trouble I'll be back. Remember one thing, Lonegan: the only piece of land that a dead man can lay claim to measures six feet deep, six feet long, and three feet wide.'

'That's big talk for a man who doesn't even carry a short gun.' Lonegan said.

'It will be there . . . if ever I should need it,' Cord answered softly.

'You're out-numbered, Cord. You really think you are going to find someone to back you up? Even if Travers and the others had nerve enough, they'd be no use to you. How do you reckon on evening up the odds?'

'By taking you out of the line-up, Lonegan. Anything happens to Mrs Corey or her daughter, and you'll find me camped near your ranch house for the rest of my life . . . or yours. Whichever comes first.'

His rifle swung suddenly, slamming into the face closing in behind him. He glanced down at the body before stepping over it. 'He won't be much use to you for a long time yet. If he's the best you got then you've got problems, Mr Lonegan.'

He paused at the door. 'Remember, Lonegan, I won't be far away. At the first sign of trouble I'll be back.'

Cord stepped quickly into the night, letting the doors swing shut behind him.

Brazos got to his feet quickly, facing Lonegan. 'If I got any wages coming, Mr Lonegan, drop it into the poor box of the church.'

'You walking out on me, Brazos?'

'No, Mr Lonegan, I'm running out on you. I don't like the odds.'

'You feeling sorry for Cord?'

'No, Mr Lonegan,' Brazos grinned. 'I'm feeling sorry for you. You hired me because I had a fast gun and a good brain. I'm using my brains now. There are already too many would-be fast guns in Boot Hill. If I'm ever passing this way again, Lonegan, I'll stop off long enough to put some fresh flowers on your grave.'

'You're yellow, Brazos. You talk a good fight, but you are nothing but a tinhorn.'

'At one time, Lonegan, I would probably have killed you for that but I'm older and wiser now. Anyhow, I figure that pleasure belongs to John Cord.'

His grin vanished as he stepped through the doors and came face to face with the man on the big Appaloosa. Quickly he lifted his hands high. 'Easy, Mr Cord. I'm not looking for trouble. I just quit.'

'I'd say that was a good decision, boy. Any particular reason?'

'Let's just say that I know something that Lonegan doesn't.' He paused. 'You told Lonegan that you are leaving the valley. That doesn't make much sense to me. The way I see it you are the only thing standing between him and what he wants. He's already making his plans. He can be waiting for you with a dozen guns by the time you come back. You won't stand a chance. By then, he'll own Triangle and the rest of the valley. You'll have no one to back you up.'

Cord looked at him, liking the boy. Unlike Brad, Brazos no longer felt he had anything to prove. He was growing up. And guns were no longer the main part of his life. Soon he would lose all his ambitions to be a fast gun, and that was a good thing.

'I won't be far away,' Cord said softly. 'It's just that I need to be by myself for a while to try to untangle my brain.'

'I'm out of a job. Need someone to watch your back? Lonegan plays dirty.'

Cord shook his head. 'If you need work, head out to Triangle. Tell Col Travers I sent you. The wages won't be what you are used to, but you'll earn them. And the food is good.'

'Thanks, Cord. There's something you should know. That kid out at Triangle . . . Brad? He's a hothead, right? Lonegan figured on pushing him into a gunfight. Thinks that way he gets the law on his side. If the kid fires the first shot, that will give Lonegan all the excuse he needs to hire a few gunhands. He'll call it protection.'

That made sense. Brad was the weak link in the chain. The boy was already itching to get that first notch on his gunbutt.

Travers would have to keep a close eye on him, keep him confined to the Triangle, if possible. Maybe Brazos could help him with that?

If Brad fired that first shot . . . He left the thought unfinished. He could already smell the gunsmoke in the air.

'Listen to Travers, Brazos. He's a good man. Tell him about Brad. Maybe he can come up with the answer.'

'I doubt it, Cord. The way I read it, kids like Brad never listen. I know: I used to be just like him.'

'What changed you, Brazos?'

'I learned there were faster guns than me about. I was lucky. The one I ran up against wasn't a very good shot.' He hesitated. 'Travers will be asking why you are not with me. What do I tell him?'

Cord felt the first raindrops brush his face as he tried to ease the tension from his body.

'Tell him I should have listened to him the first time I rode into the valley. It was good advice. Tell him I know his reasons now. He was right, there is no place for me here.'

15

He was gone. She could already sense it before she left her bedroom. The door to his room lay half-open. His bedroll was missing. She could see that without entering the room.

He had taken the coward's way out, something she had not believed him capable of, and left sometime during the night. No goodbyes. Not even a note to explain his reasons for leaving.

She swore silently. Damn him! How could he do that to her and Debbie? Didn't he realize just how much they cared about him? Did he even care about them? How could he just ride away from them without even looking back?

It took a very tough or a heartless man to do that. It would destroy Debbie when she found out that he had gone. She had worshipped John Cord.

How could any man destroy a child that way. And the hardest part of all was the fact that she would have to face Debbie with the truth.

★ ★ ★

The young man crossing the yard was a stranger to her, but he looked nice enough with an easy pleasant smile. He paused before her, lifting his hat and holding it in his hands.

'Howdy, ma'am. Thought it best I introduce myself. They call me Brazos. Col Travers hired me last night on Mr Cord's recommendation.'

'Where is Cord?' she asked bluntly.

His hesitation told her that he knew more than he was willing to tell. 'He lit out, ma'am. Didn't say where he was going. But he had a few words with Jud Lonegan before he left. Told him what he could expect if he kept pushing. I hope Lonegan was listening.'

'Did he say if he was coming back?' she asked, not really wanting an answer to her question.

'He didn't say, Mrs Corey, but I got the feeling that he had a problem to solve, and he wasn't about to find the answer down here.'

He put his hat back on as he spotted Col Travers come from the bunkhouse and stride towards them. 'Excuse me, ma'am. I've got me some work to do.'

Col Travers stopped before her, knowing the question before she asked it. 'Where is he, Col? Why did he leave?'

He shrugged. 'Who knows why a man like Cord does anything. Maybe he felt that he no longer belongs here.'

'Is he afraid of what might happen here?'

'If it comes down to gunplay, you mean? Nope. There isn't a man alive that can frighten John Cord . . . except himself. And he isn't afraid of dying.'

'Then why, Col? Why? Where is he?'

'He came face to face with something that he couldn't handle. There are no answers. And he knows it. If he stayed around here, it would destroy him and a lot of other lives. That's a chance he can't take.'

'Where is he, Trav?'

Col shrugged again, nodding towards the distant mountains. 'Up there someplace, I'd guess. Men like Cord have to be alone when there's thinking to be done.'

'Is it anything to do with that gun he keeps in his bedroll? Is that what he's running away from?'

'No man can ever escape from the shadow of the gun. Cord knows that. He tried to tell Brad, too, but Brad wasn't listening.'

'You like him, don't you, Trav?'

'I like him and admire him. Cord's a different kind of man. He can face up to every kind of challenge, except one. Right now, I wouldn't swap places with John Cord for all the gold in California. This is one fight he can't win and he knows it.'

He stopped talking as Debbie came out on to the porch; her still-sleepy eyes already searching for John Cord.

'Where's Johnny?'

Travers waited, wondering how Jane was going to handle the situation. It wouldn't be easy. How could anyone tell a child that the man she loved had walked out of her life? She would never understand Cord's reason for leaving. All the child understood was that she loved Cord and thought he loved her, too.

He watched Jane, knowing her reluctance to lie to Debbie. Well, it didn't apply to him. Anyway, lying was kinder than the truth, he decided.

'He had to leave for a while, honey,' he said easily. 'But he'll be back.'

Strangely now that the words were out of his mouth they had the ring of truth about them. John Cord would be back. He was sure of it. No matter what happened to him, John Cord couldn't hide from the truth. Even if it cost him his life.

Somehow, even as the words left Travers' mouth, Jane knew them to be the truth. But it would be a different

John Cord that rode back into the valley. And the Lord help Jud Lonegan.

She touched Debbie's shoulder, reassuring her. 'He'll be back, Debbie,' she said with conviction.

'Why didn't he say goodbye to me, tell me he was leaving?'

'He left early, Debbie. He probably didn't want to wake you up.'

'How long will he be gone?'

'Probably not long. You know how he hates being apart from you. He's told you that, hasn't he?'

'Yes, but what if he wants to leave afterwards?'

'We won't let him,' Jane said softly. 'We need him too much.'

Col Travers frowned. It was one thing to tell a lie but quite another to live one. There was no way John Cord could stay around here even if they both begged him to stay. Sooner or later, the truth would out, and it would destroy John Cord, every dream he had ever dreamed, and the lives of the couple he held most dear.

His eyes scanned the timberline. Cord was up there somewhere, a lonely, solitary man, ready to face the gun of Jud Lonegan, but reluctant to face the bitter truth of his life.

16

As usual, Sophie Coleman was up at first light. The day stretched before her, long and busy, as she moved towards the pig pen, holding her new black and white pup under her left arm. The coffee would be boiling by the time she got back to the house. The pup yelped, seeking attention. She scratched his head. The pup was a present from Col Travers. But it was unlike Travers to even think of such a thing — even if his mind wasn't cluttered by Triangle problems, so maybe it had been John Cord's idea, after all.

He would think that way.

Her eyes lifted towards the timber-line, wondering if Cord was still up there someplace, or if he had finally taken Col Travers' advice and lit out. Well, she could hardly blame him if he had. Somehow, Cord had found out the

143

reason why Travers wanted him out of the valley. It wasn't good. This was one fight that John Cord could never hope to win.

And without John Cord, the whole valley would lose. Without the threat of John Cord hanging over him Jud Lonegan would own the whole valley within a few short months. Even her small place wouldn't escape Lonegan's attention. He had aleady tried to push her off her land and would keep on trying until he succeeded.

She set her pup down, letting the tiny animal explore. Already it was showing a lot of character, bringing a smile to her face as she watched him.

Still, she couldn't watch the pup all day. There were chores to be done, stock to be fed, food to be cooked. She stooped to scratch the pup's head, before moving on to her chores. It would be another long day.

Busy with the washing, she didn't even hear the horses enter the yard. The four men were waiting as she rounded the corner of the house.

She glanced at her old buffalo gun resting on the porch.

'You won't make it,' Harvey grinned.

The fact that Harvey was along told her that she could expect an accident like the one that had happened to Len Neelson. Harvey liked fires. She glanced anxiously at her house. It wasn't much but it was home.

With a man around to do the fixing it would be a lot better. Finally she had Col Travers heading in that direction. Hell, he had even held her hand the other night. It had felt good.

'Lonegan giving you orders to shoot women now?' Sophie asked.

There was no fear in her. Lonegan wasn't ready to start a shooting war yet, but it wouldn't stop him pushing until someone else fired the first shot.

She watched Harvey dismount, his grin broad as he moved into the house. A few seconds passed before he came flying back out to land on his back in the yard, out cold.

Cully's hand dipped towards his gunbutt as John Cord appeared in the doorway, his rifle cocked and ready.

'Go ahead, mister. I enjoy killing men who go around threatening women. But you wouldn't die easy. I promise you that much. Shuck your guns before you dismount.'

Carefully, they did as they were ordered. John Cord was in a bad mood. He would kill them all without a second thought. And he could use that rifle.

'How far do you reckon it is back to Lonegan's place, Sophie?' Cord asked quietly.

' 'Bout twelve miles, I figure. A good stretch of the legs,' she smiled. 'But it ain't easy to walk in them boots they got on. Best if they left them behind. Make walking a lot easier.'

'You heard the lady,' Cord said. 'She's considerate, thinking of you that way.'

He released the horses, firing a shot into the air to send them on their way.

Sophie Coleman handed Cord a cup

of coffee before seating herself. Hitching his left hip over the porch rail, he sipped at his drink, his face thoughtful. Despite his warning, Lonegan was still pushing. No guns yet, but that would come.

'You've got pretty good timing, Cord,' Sophie said. 'I could have lost everything I have. It ain't much but it's all I got.'

'Saw them coming from a long way off. Wasn't hard to guess where they were heading for, and easy to beat them here.'

He balanced his coffee cup on the rail as he rolled a cigarette, scratching a match to life on his pants leg. Blowing smoke, he glanced around at Sophie Coleman's section of the valley. She had chosen well.

'You've got a nice place, Sophie,' he said.

'Could be a good place to be if a man ever got tired of running a big spread, and wanted a place to call his own. Think Col Travers could handle that?'

Cord nodded. 'I think so. I guess most men would like a place to call his own. With a man around to help out this would be a pretty good place to be. I guess Travers can see that.'

'How about you, Cord? You ever dream of having a place of your own?'

He drew smoke deeply into his mouth, letting it out slowly. 'Men like me are borne on the wind, Sophie. We don't belong anywhere.'

'You're in the wrong place at the wrong time, Cord. Trouble is, you are the only one who knows why you are here. You want to answer that question?'

'You wouldn't believe me, Sophie. If Pete hadn't tangled with those Indians, I'd be in Canada by now.'

'You can still ride out, Cord. Nobody will blame you for it. This is a no-win situation for you. No matter what happens here now, you lose.'

Her words still taunted him as he climbed aboard Warrior and set off again for the high country. She was right. And there would be other losers in the fight too, like Jane and Debbie. Still, it had to be. He had made his commitment and would see it through, come what may.

17

Brazos glanced at Brad as they rode toward the hollow. The kid had a pocketful of shells, and Brazos knew what that meant . . . target practice. The kid was obsessed with his gun.

Curious, Brazos had tagged along. He wanted to see just how good Brad was with a gun. He had the feeling that he was nothing more than a blowhard, but that would have to be seen.

He shook his head slowly. He had seen too many kids like Brad. Hell, he had been just like him a few years back, but he had learned the hard way. He had been lucky. Billy Trace's shooting had been a little off the day he had faced him.

Maybe Brad wouldn't be so lucky!

Still, it was one thing to be able to pull a gun, but quite another to be able to kill a man. That split-second of indecision in pulling a trigger could make the difference between life and death. He wondered if Brad really had it in him to kill a man. There was only one way to find out, and Brazos hoped he wouldn't be around if it came down to it.

A cocky grin spread across Brad's face as his gun swept up into his hand and a tin can leapt into the air. Three hits out of five. Not bad, but there was still that slight hesitation between pulling the gun and shooting.

Still the kid was pretty good, better than Brazos could hope to be, but then Brazos had long since given up practising. He had no intention of becoming the fastest gun in Boot Hill. Taking a gun job with Lonegan had been nothing more than a bluff. At the first sign of trouble, Brazos' intention had always been to saddle up and ride away.

'Well, Brazos, you've been around. How do you think I'd do against the top guns?'

'Only a fool sets off to kill a man because of a reputation, Brad. Most of the top guns I know avoid each other. There's no glory in being second best . . . only death.'

'I ain't afraid to face up to anyone. I'm not afraid to carry a gun or use it. And I don't run away from anything or anyone.'

'Meaning Johnny Cord? It's my bet that he isn't running, that he's still around here someplace, and he'll be back when the time is right. There's more to being a gunfighter than being able to use a gun, Brad. You have to be able to read men. Knowing when to back off can save your life. Just because a man doesn't carry a gun, doesn't mean he's scared or can't use it. Remember one thing, Bearcat Riley thought Cord was easy meat, but he was wrong. He was lucky — he's still living. You make the same mistake and it could prove fatal.'

He swung back into the saddle, wheeling the roan before glancing down at Brad. 'You need a lot more practice before going up against any of the top guns. Remember something else, too, it's easy to pull a gun but not so easy to kill a man. And the top guns have had a lot more practice at that than you have.'

* * *

Hearing the rapid gunfire, Cord reined in Warrior. He knew just where that sound was coming from, and just what it meant. Brad was back behind his gun again, proving to himself, or others, just how good he was. The kid was a fool, didn't know what he was getting himself into.

The kid already had everything that most gunfighters would give their right arms for — a home, family, someone to care about them. But Brad was willing to throw all that away just to build himself a reputation.

Once a man stepped into the shadow of the gun there was no getting out. No peace. No place to hide from that shadow. There was always someone like Brad coming along, eager young punks waiting to take that reputation from you. And someday that would happen. It always happened.

There would be no one to mourn the passing of John Cord, no one to even know he was dead. That was a good thing; at least, someone would be spared that much pain.

He heeled Warrior forward, heading him towards the high country, once more feeling the need for the solitude that only the hills could bring him. It was a feeling that had always been with him and he wondered if he would ever lose it. He wished he could follow that urge all the way to Canada but knew he couldn't. Trouble was coming to the valley and there was no way that he could avoid it.

Brad would light the fuse. He would make the first mistake and John Cord would have to be there to pull his irons out of the fire. A lot of kids like Brad had made that first mistake and most of them lived just long enough to regret it.

Brad would kill his first man, or die trying. There was no way of telling if the kid had nerve enough to pull the trigger after pulling the gun, until the time came. Then the whole valley would erupt into violence, and there was nothing that John Cord could do to stop it.

More than one man would die that day. John Cord would die that day, too.

In his place would appear a man more terrible than anyone could imagine . . . a man he had long since buried, and hoped never to see again.

18

The evening shadows were lengthening as Debbie said goodnight to Pinto and moved back towards the house, stopping to watch the sun go down. She liked to watch the sun set, even though it reminded her that bedtime was near. As usual, she found herself searching the distance for the familiar sight of the tall man atop the big Appaloosa.

Something moved in the distance, a shadow only, but she found herself holding her breath. There was no mistaking him now. John Cord was back and she found herself yelling with joy. He hadn't deserted her after all. He loved her too much to ever leave her, she could tell.

Her sudden yell brought her mother rushing from the house as she wondered what Debbie was yelling for. Her face, too, broke into a happy smile as she recognized John Cord. He was back, just as she always knew he would. Debbie and she had become a part of his life that he could never really leave behind.

Light rain fell as they rushed forward to greet him. He left Warrior ground-hitched as he stooped and lifted Debbie high into the air, giving her a warm kiss on the cheek before setting her down again. He looked embarrassed as he faced Jane. Such shows of affection were alien to John Cord.

'It's good to have you back,' Jane said warmly. It was the truth. The ranch, despite being her home for all her life, had seemed a cold and empty place without him around. Debbie had felt it, too.

'Where is everyone?' he asked.

'Travers and the others are out on the range. Brad and Brazos are in town. Col figured it was safe for them to go in now that Bearcat is out of the way.'

She stopped talking at the look on his face. 'It's OK. Col told them to leave their guns behind.'

'Was anyone listening?' Cord asked softly.

It was one thing to tell Brad what to do, something else to get him to do it. Just because Brad didn't have a gun with him, didn't mean he couldn't get his hands on one. Any one of Lonegan's men would be glad to loan Brad a gun.

Still Brazos was with him. He had a cool head and could, maybe, keep Brad in check. It was the best he could hope for. He swore silently. Even with Brazos he didn't trust Brad out of his sight. The kid had a hair-trigger temper and the last thing the valley needed right now was a hothead with a gun in his hand.

'There's coffee on the stove,' Jane said quietly.

He nodded his thanks. 'I'll just take care of Warrior and I'll be right in.'

As usual, Debbie was at his side, closer than ever as if she was afraid he was going to disappear from her life again as he led Warrior into the stables.

'You are not going to leave me again are you, Johnny?' she asked fearfully. 'Please don't leave me again.'

'I never want to leave you, sweetheart. Always remember that, but sometimes things happen that we have no control over. You'll understand that when you are older. Never forget something else. No matter what happens I'll always love you.'

There was no way she was going to take her eyes off him as she watched him unsaddle Warrior, rub him down and feed him. Every action was etched into her memory as she studied him. Johnny was her friend. He wouldn't leave her again. Of course, he hadn't given his word, but somehow she knew.

Cord sipped at his coffee, his third cup. Debbie had gone to bed, after getting his promise that he would still be here when she got up in the morning. He wished he could promise that for all his tomorrows but couldn't. For him, all his tomorrows were uncertain.

He was aware of Jane watching him, knowing that he had something to say but didn't know how. There were always a lot of unspoken words when two people felt as they did about each other. In their case perhaps the words were best left unsaid.

'We have to talk, Johnny,' she said suddenly. 'You know how Debbie and I feel about you, but we don't know how to live with the knowledge that someday you will ride away from us. We don't want to live with that fact. We need you here with us forever.'

'I can't make that promise, Jane,' he said quietly. 'I am what I am. I made my mistake a long time ago and I can't wipe it out.'

'Does it have anything to do with that gun in your bedroll? I found it one day when I went to do some laundry and sewing for you.'

He nodded.

'The gun can stay in your bedroll, Johnny. It doesn't have to come out again. No one need ever know about it.'

'I'll know, Jane. You can take the gun from the man, but you can't take the man from the gun. I've lived in its shadow ever since the day I strapped it on. There is no escape.'

'That's the thing that you've tried to get Brad to understand, isn't it, Johnny? But he isn't listening because you aren't wearing a gun to back up your words.'

'Brad is going to have to learn the hard way, Jane. Too bad someone has to die before he learns that lesson.'

'If you stayed around, Johnny, perhaps he would start listening to you.'

'It wouldn't work, Jane. Even without the gun I'd still have to ride the wind. Men like me don't belong anyplace.'

'And Debbie and me, don't we mean anything to you? Can you just ride away from us without even looking back?'

'You mean more to me than you will ever know. The only reason I can ride away from here is because I have to. I was playing against a stacked deck from the moment I rode into the valley, but I didn't know it. That's the one thing that

I can't beat. All I can do now is try to make up for it. I owe you all that much. Words . . . '

The sound of hoofbeats in the yard distracted him and he stopped talking. He was rolling a cigarette when Col Travers strolled into the house his eyes searching for Brad. He exchanged brief nods with Cord but there was little doubt that he was glad to see the tall man back. At least, it meant that Jane and Debbie weren't left unprotected when he was out on the range. Still, there was no sign of Brad and that bothered him.

'Brad back yet?' he asked abruptly. The kid had been gone a long time and he didn't like it. The kid had a hot temper and a low tolerance for drink. That was a bad combination.

The fact that Brazos was with the kid helped ease his worry. With a bit of luck, Brazos would be able to keep the kid on a tight rein, but there was still doubts. Brad didn't like taking orders from anyone.

The kid was just waiting for someone to light his fuse, and any one of Lonegan's men was ready and willing to light it. Brazos had already warned him about that.

'He wasn't wearing his gun when he rode out, Col,' Jane told him.

He glanced at Cord. There were still doubts in the tall man; just because Brad wasn't wearing his gun when he rode out, it didn't mean that he didn't have it with him.

Reading the tall man's thoughts, Col said 'I'll check.'

Cord got to his feet, reaching for his rifle hanging on pegs high out of Debbie's reach. He was getting that bad feeling, too.

'I'll saddle Warrior.'

Travers had already disappeared through the door. Cord was heading in the same direction when she stepped before him.

'What is it? What's wrong?' A sudden thought struck her. 'You think he's got his gun in his saddlebags or

163

bedroll, don't you?'

Cord shrugged. 'We'll know for sure when Travers gets back.'

'Do you really think Brad is capable of killing a man?'

'Most men can kill if they get pushed hard enough. Believe me, Lonegan will do all the pushing if he sees Brad wearing a gun, and the kid is too dumb to know any better.'

The door opened again and he caught Travers' brief nod. The kid was in town and it was a sure bet that the kid was wearing his gun. There could be no other reason for taking it with him.

'I've got one of the boys saddling Warrior for you, Cord,' Travers said. 'Maybe we can still make it in time.'

Jane stared at both men, unwilling or unable to believe her ears. It was her son they were talking about, someone who was about to kill or get himself killed — if it hadn't already happened. The thought filled her with dread.

Cord already had the bad feeling that they were too late. The second that

Lonegan noticed Brad was wearing a gun, he would cut his men loose.

Cord's face tightened. By now, one or more men were dead. Either way, they were too late. By wearing his gun to town, Brad had already unleashed the violence that would engulf the whole valley. But maybe Brad would never know of the trouble he had caused. By now, Brad could already be dead.

19

Cord was slipping his Winchester into his saddle sheath when he heard the sound of hoofbeats. He turned quickly, the rifle sliding back into his hands. Two horses coming fast.

He waited. Brad's grin as he reined his horse to a stop chilled him. He knew what that grin meant. He glanced at Brazos' face for confirmation. Damn! Brad had finally lit that fuse.

The kid dismounted, facing Travers and Cord with his hands on his hips. 'You can take one of Lonegan's men out of the line-up. He wasn't good enough.'

'Not this one,' Travers said quietly, 'but maybe the next one will be. You were told to leave your gun behind when you went to town, Brad.'

'I got tired of backing up, Travers. They had to know that there is at least one man riding for the Triangle. They'll think twice now before trying to push us around again.'

Ignoring him, Cord turned his attention to Brazos. 'Who was he?'

'Nobody. They called him Taco. I guess they just kept him around for laughs. They used to kid him that he was the toughest guy around, and the fastest gun that ever lived. Everyone used to act scared whenever he was about. I don't think Taco ever really believed it, but he went along with it. One of the boys turned him loose on Brad when they saw him wearing a gun. I guess it started off as a joke, but Brad wasn't laughing. He killed Taco. The poor ox didn't have a chance.'

'He had his chance, Brazos, but he wasn't good enough. None of them are. Lonegan knows better than to mess with me now.'

Cord looked at him. 'So you are a real gunfighter now, Brad. You've just killed your first man. Maybe he wasn't much of a man but he was more then than he is now. Right now, he's nothing more than a notch on your gunbutt. That's all any of them will ever be. Most of the time you won't even know their names, and that's the only way you can ever live with it. That's the way you will end up, too, Brad, nothing more than a notch on someone else's gunbutt.'

'That will never happen, Cord. I'm the best. Nobody is ever going to take me out. Nobody.'

Jane watched horrified as Cord's hand lashed out suddenly, driving Brad off his feet. Moving quickly, the tall man's foot clamped down on Brad's right hand as he reached for his gun.

Pain flashed across her son's face but she held firm. The fact that Brad had just killed a man — her own son — bothered her, but John Cord was the best man to handle the situation. Travers had tried to handle Brad but failed. Now it was up to Cord. Sooner or later, he would force Brad to listen to him.

Cord increased the pressure on Brad's hand. The kid was in pain but he didn't care. The kid had lit the powder keg that would blow this valley to hell and gone. There would be others feeling a lot more pain than Brad before this thing was over.

'I could make it easy for you, Brad. I could cripple you here and now, but I don't want to make life too easy for you. Anyway it's too late now. You've given Lonegan the licence to hire as many gunfighters as he needs. You killed more than one man tonight, boy.'

He glanced at Brazos. 'The man he killed . . . he have any kind of family?'

Brazos shrugged. 'Seem to recall something about a sister back in Kansas, but I can't be sure.'

Cord took his foot off Brad's hand and stepped back. 'That make any difference to you, Brad?'

'None at all, Cord. He had his chance but he wasn't good enough. That goes for anyone who goes up against me.' His eyes blazed with anger as he glared at him. 'Maybe you'd like to try your luck against me?'

'It's an interesting thought, Brad,' Cord said softly. 'But, unlike you, I don't like the idea of killing anyone.'

'You wouldn't even come close,' Brad snarled, as he began setting up tin cans on the corral fence. If Lonegan started hiring gunfighters he would need as much practice as he could get. Not that it would make much difference, he could take out any gun that Lonegan set against him. He was the best, and he would prove it.

Someday, he promised himself, he would meet up with Jack Bodell, and he would prove himself the best ever.

Cord shook his head sadly as he gathered up Warrior's reins to lead him back into the stables. Brad had killed his first man and was proud of it. The fool had put everyone in the valley under threat, including his own family, and was too stupid to realize it.

By now, Lonegan would be sending

out word that he was hiring gunslingers. But he would only be hiring the best. You could bet on that. Lonegan had already been waiting too long to own this valley.

Who? The question floated in his mind as he unsaddled Warrior. Jim Fallon? It was a pretty good bet. Fallon was closest — last time he had heard. Morey Laine? Another good bet. Both men were good with a gun, high among the best.

Another name sprang to his mind. Caleb Towney! So far it was only a name, but he had a big reputation. Some said he was faster than Jack Bodell had ever been. And colder. If Towney had ever had a human emotion they said he kept it well hidden.

It didn't matter to Towney how he killed a man just as long as that man died. Most men, even known gunfighters, avoided Caleb Towney. The man was a cold, emotionless killer, and didn't care who his victims were. Some said he had wiped out an entire family when riding in the Lincoln County war, but there were no witnesses.

Those who knew him accepted the story as fact.

He hesitated as he untied his bedroll, holding it in his hands as he heard the familiar sound of gunfire. Despite his mother's protests, Brad was determined to show the other hands just how good he was with a gun. A man had died tonight because of Brad's urge to show off. That was no good reason to kill anyone.

There was never a good reason.

★   ★   ★

Brad grinned as he reloaded. He liked being the centre of attention. Right now, he was showing everyone how good he was with a gun, and even Travers looked impressed. Too bad Cord wasn't here to see it. The tall man was still hiding in the stables. Hell, even talking about gunplay upset John Cord.

The man was gunshy. No doubt

about that. John Cord was just plain scared of guns, and had probably never even pulled a gun in his life.

The tall man's shadow fell over him, but he didn't turn around. 'My shooting bother you, Cord? The way I see it now, you ain't got but two choices — you either cut and run again or get yourself a gun.'

'I already got a gun,' said Cord.

The sudden hush following his word told Brad he was speaking the truth. He turned slowly, his eyes drawn to the black, mother-of-pearl-gripped Colt. The gun hung easily on Cord's right hip as if it belonged there — a part of the man.

'Nice-looking gun, Cord. Maybe if you asked me I'd even give you lessons in how to use it.'

'I was hoping you'd say that, Brad,' Cord said quietly. It seemed that everything the tall man did was understated. 'Set them up again, Trav. Brad is going to teach me how to use a gun.'

'You sure you want to do this, Cord?' Travers asked. 'There are other ways to handle this.'

'Not for Brad. Brad always has to learn things the hard way. Call it whenever you want, boy. Don't wait for me.'

'I wasn't about to, Cord. I ain't got that much time to spare.'

The words were hardly out of his mouth before his hand dipped, hoping to catch the tall man unawares, but Cord's gun was already blazing before he could clear leather. He swore. Cord had already cleared the top rail, and Brad no longer had any targets to shoot at.

He felt the blood drain from his face. Cord had made him look like a fool, shamed him in front of everyone. He had made the first move but Cord had beaten him easily, made him look slow.

Travers was right about John Cord. He had tried to warn Brad about Cord the first time the tall stranger had ridden in with Pete's body, but he hadn't been listening then. Still refused to listen until now. It had taken John Cord himself to show him how wrong he was.

Cord was good. Probably the best. And no matter how hard he tried, or how much he practised, he would always live in John Cord's shadow. He knew that now. It was a bitter pill to swallow, but he would always be second best. There was an ease with which Cord used a gun that he could never hope to reach.

'How did you get so good with a gun, Cord?' he asked angrily. Despite the fact that he was seeing Cord in a new light, he didn't like being made a fool of.

'You are not the first kid to make a mistake, Brad,' Cord said quietly, as he reloaded. 'Maybe you'll be lucky and it will end right here for you.'

'And if it doesn't?'

'Then you'll spend the rest of your life regretting the day you first strapped on a gunbelt. How long that life will be depends upon just how smart you are.'

He dropped the big Colt back into leather, and started back towards the stables.

'Now, Cord!' Brad yelled suddenly.

His hand dipped towards his gun. He wanted to test the tall man again, find out just how good the man was. He recoiled in shock as he found himself covered by the muzzle of that black Colt. God! He hadn't even seen the tall man's hand move. Nobody could be that fast.

For the first time in his life he felt fear, a cold hand gripping his insides, as he saw the look on Cord's face. He was a bare half-second away from death.

A slight tremor rippled through Cord's body as he holstered his gun. 'That was a fool stunt, boy. Playing games with guns could get you killed.'

He turned abruptly and walked into the stables, leaving Brad ashen-faced and weak. That close. It had been that close.

'Now you know how easy it is to get

yourself killed, Brad,' Travers said quietly.

'You knew how good he was, Travers. You always knew, but you let me go right ahead and make a fool of myself.'

'I warned you, Brad. I warned you about John Cord the first time he rode into the valley, but you weren't listening. You listening now? Maybe there's hope for you yet, Brad. You just admitted being a fool. Maybe that means you are finally growing up.'

He paused to roll a smoke, watching the rest of the hands return to the bunkhouse. They would have a lot to talk about. Jane still waited on the porch, her face taut. Like Travers, she hadn't wanted to see John Cord resort to gunplay.

'You made a couple of mistakes tonight, boy. Because you didn't follow my orders and leave your gun behind when you rode to town, a man died. A man died, Brad, but the only thing you felt was pride because you had beaten him to the draw. I bet John Cord didn't feel that way the first time he killed a man. I bet he felt sick to his stomach . . . bet he felt that way every time he was forced to kill a man. Because of you, Brad, he may be forced to kill other men, and he'll still feel that way. Killing will never come easy to John Cord.'

'He can always run away again,' Brad snapped.

'There's only one thing John Cord ever ran away from, Brad, but that's the one thing he can't escape from.'

The anger still boiled in Brad. Cord had made him look and feel like a fool kid. And that wouldn't be easy to forget or forgive.

'Why don't you share that information with us, Travers? What is Cord running from?'

'Himself, boy,' Travers said quietly.

20

Heedless of his horse's heaving flanks or his pain, Coby reined the gelding to a brutal halt. It had been a long, fast ride from town, but that didn't matter. There was always another horse. He had news that Lonegan would be glad to hear.

Leaving the horse free, Coby hammered on the door. Lonegan liked everyone to knock before entering his house, and any man who did not follow Lonegan's orders soon found himself without a job.

Right now, Coby needed a job. The money was good.

He entered quickly without waiting for Lonegan's permission. This was one time the big man wouldn't mind. As usual, he was seated near the fire in his big armchair sipping at his brandy. Good quality stuff, too. Lonegan always had a taste for quality.

He was glaring at Coby now. 'I hope you have a good reason for pushing your way in like this, Coby?'

'I think so. You got your wish tonight. The Corey kid came into town packing a gun.'

The news pleased the big man. A smile spread across his face; a rare sight that, Coby thought. Lonegan got his only pleasure from having power.

'And?'

'Some of the boys got Taco to brace him. Taco lost. I figured we'd bury him here on the ranch.'

Lonegan's smile spread. That was good news. Taco's death had served a purpose . . . probably the only worthwhile thing the fool had done in his whole life. There were no regrets at the man's death.

'How good with a gun is that kid?' he asked.

'Pretty good. I guess he could make a living as a gunfighter — for a short time.'

The fact that Brad Corey wasn't as good with a gun as the kid thought he was pleased Lonegan. A real fast gun could have put a crimp in his plans. If the kid had been any good with a gun it could have given the ranchers fresh heart, someone to stand behind when the trouble started. To be sure they wouldn't be standing in front of Brad Corey when it came to a showdown.

He laughed aloud. When the real fast guns came in to the valley, they would be working for him, and the man he had in mind would frighten the hell out of most of the ranchers without a shot being fired. Only the Triangle would have nerve enough to stand against them, but not for long. They wouldn't stand a snowball in Hell's chance. It would be the Alamo all over again.

His smile reappeared as he reached for the small silver bell at his side. Within seconds a little Mexican appeared, his head bowed.

'Brandy, Coby?' Lonegan asked.

Coby nodded, unable to believe his

ears. For the first time ever Lonegan had offered him a drink. His news had really pleased the big man. He could now take over the valley any time he wanted to.

Lonegan waited until the little Mexican had disappeared before speaking again. 'Then the kid is our only real problem but nothing that can't be handled. Any real fast gun could take him out. Someone like Fallon, perhaps?'

Coby nodded agreement, before taking a sip at his drink. He had to take advantage of the situation. It was very unlikely that Lonegan would ever offer him a drink again. He wasn't a brandy drinker, but had to admit the stuff was smooth.

'Thinking of hiring Fallon?'

'His name came up, but I've got someone else in mind. You've been around, Coby. I hear you ran with a wild bunch before I hired you. It seems to me that you know a lot more about gunfighters than I do. I want names.

Suggestions. I want to own this valley as soon as possible.'

Coby shrugged. 'I've seen most of them,' he admitted. 'You've already mentioned Fallon. Then there's Morey Laine. Knew him once. I'd say he was even faster than Fallon, and meaner.'

The name of Caleb Towney came to his mind, but he was reluctant to speak it. The man wasn't human . . . didn't care who his victims were — men, women or children. Towney took an inhuman satisfaction in killing.

Hell, even the thought of Towney made him shudder.

'Who else?' Lonegan prompted.

'Jack Bodell! But nobody's heard of him for a long time. Most people reckon he's dead. Even if he wasn't, he wouldn't be for sale. Bodell never hired his gun in his life.'

'Sounds as if you admire him, Coby?'

'Never set eyes on him, but they say he was the best. Never killed a man who didn't ask for it or deserved to die. The fact is Bodell walked away from more fights than any other gunfighter I ever heard of.'

'There's one name you haven't mentioned, Coby, Caleb Towney. Is there something about him that bothers you?'

'Everything. Towney isn't human. I guess he's never had a decent thought or emotion in his life. He just likes to kill, and it doesn't matter to him who the victim is. Hell! Turn him loose here and he'd wipe out everyone in the valley.'

'It won't come to that, Coby. All he needs, all we need, is his reputation. The day he rides into the valley, everyone will start packing up and moving out.'

'It won't be that way, Mr Lonegan. Nobody can control Towney. He's crazy. You hire him, and you give him a licence to kill every one who crosses his path. I've seen what he's capable of and I want no part of it.'

'I can control Towney, Coby. We go back a long way . . . all the way back to the war when Towney developed a taste for killing. I gave him orders then; he'll still follow my orders now. When I crack the whip he will still jump.'

'The war ended a long time ago, Mr Lonegan. Most men came home from it with a real sickening of killing. But not Caleb Towney. Killing was the only real pleaure he got from life. It still is. You turn him loose in this valley and nobody will be safe. He wiped out an entire family during the Lincoln County war, they say, and never gave it a second thought.'

'There are always victims in any kind of war,' Lonegan said, 'and only one winner. I intend to be that winner.'

'I took part in the war, too, Lonegan. I didn't like killing then and I don't like it now. Taco died tonight because he was pushed into a fight he couldn't hope to win. The boys egged him into that fight, on your orders. Taco's dead but you don't give a damn. He served his purpose. That leaves you one man short, Lonegan. You hire Caleb Towney and that will leave you two men short. I don't want to be around when he rides into this valley.'

'I'll have your wages ready for you come morning,' Lonegan said flatly. 'I have no use for a coward.'

Coby moved towards the door, stopping with his hand on the handle. 'There's another name I didn't mention, Lonegan, John Cord.'

Lonegan grinned. 'Cord? He doesn't even carry a gun. What makes you think he's so dangerous?'

'Call it a hunch. Some men walk soft, talk soft, but throw a big shadow. I think Cord is such a man. The day he rode into the Triangle you lost any hope of ever owning this valley. And I don't think Morey Laine, Jim Fallon or Caleb Towney will stop him.'

21

A light rain misted the air as Cord dismounted and loosened Warrior's cinches. Leaving the big horse ground-hitched, he squatted on his heels, rolling a smoke with his usual long-practised ease, his eyes intent on the far distant mountains.

His past was already catching up with him again, and Jane and Brad had caught a glimpse of the real John Cord last night. He hadn't liked doing that. The big, black Colt had been a part of his past and should have remained that way, but Brad had a lesson to be learned, and he knew of no other way to do it.

It took only one mistake to set off on the wrong trail. By killing Taco, Brad could already have set off on that trail. He hoped not. He knew that trail . . . had travelled it ever since he was a

187

seventeen-year-old kid. It was a short trail — leading straight to Hell.

Born with a natural skill, a quick hand, steady nerves and a sharp eye, using a gun had come easy for Cord, but he had never looked for trouble. He had even tried backing away from his first gunfight, but the man had kept pushing until he had no choice. That face had haunted him for a long time after. Unlike Brad, he had taken no pleasure in killing his first man or any man since.

The shadows were lengthening when he heard the sound of hoofbeats, and turned quietly, whistling softly to Warrior. The big horse obeyed quickly, coming to his side, stopping long enough for Cord to lift out his rifle from the saddle sheath, and swiftly untie his bedroll, before moving away from the tall man into the shelter of the nearby trees.

Cord's eyes fastened on the lone rider, relaxing as he recognized Jane. There was no urgency in the way she rode, but she was alert and watchful as she sought him out.

She smiled as she reined the bay gelding to a halt. 'You are a hard man to find, John Cord,' she said, as he helped her dismount.

The promise of rain had died. Long shafts of golden light slashed across the valley. It was a beautiful evening, she decided, as she faced the tall man. It was the first time they had been really alone. Debbie had always been nearby, usually sleeping, but she had always been there.

'She's at home with Brad,' she said in answer to his unspoken question. 'He's spent most of the day hanging around the house. I think he finally realizes what it's like to take another man's life, understands what it really means.'

She paused, studying his stern face. Cord was a man used to hiding his emotions, but she knew what he was thinking.

'You taught Brad a lesson last night. It was a rough lesson, but I think he learned something important.'

'I was a bit rough on him,' he admitted, 'but I knew of no other way to get him to see what he was doing to himself and others. You can't restore a man's life. When a man sets out to build himself a reputation as a gunfighter there is no turning back. It would have been a short career for Brad.'

'I know, Johnny,' she said quietly. 'And I think Brad does too. I don't think he's quite ready to accept that fact yet, but he knows.'

She hesitated. All this talk of guns and gunfighters upset her, but it was worse for Cord. They had been a part of his life for too long. And it wasn't ended yet.

Because of a brash kid, Cord had been forced to buckle on a gun again last night. The next time he strapped on a gun someone would die. There was nothing more certain than that. The thought that it might be John Cord sickened her and filled her with dread.

There was more to be said, something he had to know. 'Brazos was looking for you . . . said he had a message for you.'

He looked at her. It wasn't difficult. There was nothing he enjoyed more than looking at her. Those blue-green eyes held a special wonder for him.

'I told him that I would find you, give you the message. He said . . . said that Lonegan was hiring guns. Coby told him. Coby made a point of meeting up with Brazos and giving him the news before he rode out. He told Brazos that he had quit Lonegan because he didn't like what was happening.'

'He mention any names?' Cord asked flatly.

It had started just as he knew it would. He glanced at his bedroll. Soon that black Colt would be back around his waist again, but this time he wouldn't be shooting at tin cans.

She was watching him, reading his mind. 'It's all Brad's fault, isn't it?'

He shook his head. 'Things had to

come to a head sooner or later. Brad was just the excuse that Lonegan needed. If it hadn't been him, he would have found another excuse to start gunplay.'

He looked at her again, knowing she was still avoiding his last question.

'Brazos mention any names?' he asked again.

Again that slight hesitation. 'Jim Fallon. Morey Laine.'

Cord frowned. Lonegan didn't believe in half measures. Either Fallon or Laine would be enough to frighten half the population from the valley, but togther. Lonegan meant business. That much was sure.

He looked at her again, sensing she was holding something back. 'What else, Jane? You aren't telling me everything.'

'There was one other name . . . Caleb Towney. I'm afraid, Johnny. I've heard his name before. He's evil, pure evil.'

Cord's face tightened. Caleb Towney!

No man in his right mind would even consider hiring someone like Towney. The man was beyond control, nothing more than a crazy killer. Turn him loose in this valley and there was no telling what would happen.

'Why would Lonegan hire Towney?'

'Brazos asked Coby the same question. It seems that Towney rode under Lonegan during the war. It was the only time that Towney ever followed orders. Lonegan thinks he can still control him.'

'It says something about Lonegan, too,' Cord said softly. 'Towney rode with Bloody Bill Anderson during the war. If Lonegan was giving him orders that means he rode with the same outfit. Not many men will admit to that. It seems that Mr Lonegan knows how to kill, too, and he isn't too particular about his victims, either.'

'How good is Towney with a gun, Johnny?'

'Never seen him in action, but I hear he's good, very good. I've seen him once or twice, but always kept out of his way. Towney is the kind of trouble that nobody needs.'

'Do you think he's as good with a gun as Jack Bodell?' she asked fearfully.

He shrugged, his mind elsewhere. Fallon and Laine were bad news in anyone's language, but Caleb Towney was something else. The man was quite capable of wiping out the entire valley on his own and not showing one hint of remorse.

'Some say he's even better,' he answered thoughtlessly, before the full intent of her question hit him.

He looked at her quickly, noting the tear-filled eyes at his answer and the trembling of her body.

Damn! This wasn't the way it should have been. He should have stayed in the valley long enough to take care of Lonegan before riding out again. Maybe he should have strapped on his gun and called out Lonegan and the others that night in the saloon. It would have been a lot easier then.

Now, with Towney and the others coming in, things would be a lot harder. There was a good chance that he wouldn't survive, he admitted to himself. The thought didn't bother him. He had no future anyway.

'How long have you known?' he asked quietly.

'Since the night of the dance. I've kept a diary ever since I was a young girl. Everything that has ever happened to me is written in those diaries — all my dreams, plans, hopes and fears. In one of those diaries I wrote of a shy young cowboy that I saw at a Saturday night dance. He had disappeared the next morning but I needed a name for that diary. I thought of making one up, but then I thought of the hotel. There were five names registered in the hotel that night, only one of them I knew, so that left four. I tried describing you but the hotel clerk was still too drunk to even remember registering anyone, so I wrote all those names in my diary. Of course, I couldn't even be sure that you had slept in the hotel. For all I knew, you could have spent a night in the stable loft. I forgot those names until last night when I saw you using a gun. Afterwards, I went through all my old diaries until I found the one I was looking for and only one name made sense.'

'And you don't hate me?' he asked slowly.

'I could never hate you, Johnny. I feel the same way about you that Debbie does.'

'That could change, Jane, when she learns the truth about me.'

'There had to be a reason for what happened, Johnny. There is always a reason for everything you do.'

'Then you'll know my reason for riding out when this is all over?'

'You can ride out now, Johnny. No one will ever blame you for it.'

'Debbie will,' he said softly.

'I'll explain everything to her, Johnny. She loves you enough to understand.'

'Will you explain everything, Jane?' he asked flatly.

'I don't know what happened that night, Johnny. Only you and Col Travers know that. Do you want to talk about it?'

He shook his head. 'It won't change anything.'

'You can always come back when this is over,' she said quietly.

He shook his head again. 'A man can ride away from his future, Jane. But he can never ride away from his past.'

22

Jonas moved quickly from his usual seat on the boardwalk outside the saloon as he spotted the thin, white-haired man riding down the street astride a tired, skinny, roan horse. Pale, almost colourless eyes looked at Jonas, dismissing him quickly as he dismounted.

Jonas felt a chill through his body. There was no mistaking Caleb Towney. There was an aura of real evil about the man. He waited until Towney had entered the saloon before moving away quickly. He wanted to be as far away as possible. Any man with sense liked a lot of distance between him and Caleb Towney.

Still, this was news that John Cord would want to hear. With luck he could borrow a horse at the livery and ride out to give Cord the news. Strangely enough, he felt the news wouldn't worry Cord too much. The man had a steel in him that few, if any, had.

Even if Towney was a faster gun than Cord, he had the feeling that Cord wouldn't die until he killed Towney.

Fallon and Morey Laine glanced up as Towney entered the saloon, looking away quickly. The man was a brute, a man without feelings of any kind. But, unlike most men, Towney had never sought a reputation. He just liked to kill. Nothing else mattered to him.

Even the sight of Caleb Towney sickened most men. Fallon could already feel the bile rising in his throat. If he had known Towney was involved, he would have stayed well away. Maybe it wasn't too late to ride out now, but money was in short supply, and Fallon liked money.

As usual, Towney chose to sit alone with his back to the wall, a bottle and glass before him on the table. If he was aware of Jim Fallon or Morey Laine, he gave no indication. Towney liked his own company, trusting no man. Keeping his back to the wall made a lot of sense; there were a lot of men, women too, waiting in line to get a shot at Towney. And nobody would ever blame them.

Fallon poured another drink to kill the bitter taste in his mouth. It didn't help. There was a smell, too, the stench of death that Caleb Towney always carried with him.

There were rumours that Towney had started his killing career during the war under Bloody Bill Anderson, but Fallon couldn't be certain about that. Towney never talked about himself; never talked much, anyway.

It was said that he had served under a captain who took almost as much pleasure from killing as he did. What had happened to that captain after the war ended nobody knew for sure, but Fallon had the feeling that he was still around.

He glanced at Laine. They had never been friends, but had ridden together a few times. If Laine shared his disgust of

Caleb Towney he showed no indication of it, but then Morey had always been a cold emotional man, too.

Fallon relaxed a little as two men entered the saloon, the smaller of the two holding the door open for the bigger man. So this was Jud Lonegan. had to be ... the man was too well dressed and too arrogant to be a nobody.

He turned at the sound of a chair moving back and was surprised to find Towney on his feet, standing to attention almost. He had been right, after all. Towney was still under his captain's command. For Towney the war had never ended.

Lonegan was still giving orders and Towney still obeying them. It said a lot about Lonegan, too, that Towney was still willing to take orders from him. What was the name of that captain again? He searched his memory but nothing came. It would come back when it was ready. But one thing was sure ... he would have to walk carefully around both Towney and Lonegan now. Both men were dangerous and of uncertain temper.

He swore silently. Coming here had been a mistake. He could feel it now, but there was no backing out. Once a hired gun backed away from a fight, his career was finished.

Lonegan nodded briefly at Towney before seating himself facing the two men. Stroud would watch his back, standing between him and the door. Since Corby's departure, Stroud had moved up the totem pole becoming his right-hand man.

He waited for Towney to move his chair forward to join them before speaking. 'You know why you are here. When I want a job done I hire only the best. Caleb I know. There's a job to be done, and you are the men to do it. I hired you for your reputations. Don't let me down.'

He poured himself a drink from the bottle that Stroud brought from the bar. 'I intend owning every blade of grass in this valley, and I hired you to help me get it.'

'That's a pretty tall order, Mr Lonegan,' Fallon said softly. 'I'd guess there are a lot of people in this valley.'

'Only one thing stands in my way, the Triangle. Once they fold, the rest will follow suit. It will be all mine then.'

'That still doesn't tell me what I'm up against. How many guns, Mr Lonegan?'

'Frightened of something, Fallon?' Towney asked. His pale eyes challenged Fallon, but Fallon wasn't biting.

'Just like to know what the odds are, Towney,' Fallon said.

Lonegan nodded. 'I like a man who weighs up the odds before jumping in feet first. There's only one fast gun in the valley, at least, he thinks so. His mother owns the Triangle. He killed one of my men a few days ago. That's the reason I sent for you. When a man works for me, I own him. And I don't like losing anything I own. There is always a price to pay for anyone who crosses me. You men will see that Brad Corey pays that price. He fired the first shot in the valley. I'll fire the last.'

'Sounds easy,' Fallon said gently. 'But if it's that easy why do you need three of us?'

'I want everyone to see that I mean business.'

'This Corey,' Morey Laine said for the first time, 'how good is he with a gun?'

'About half as good as he thinks he is. He's just a hot-headed kid. Any one of you could take him out without any trouble. My biggest problem is Col Travers. He's holding the other ranchers together. The kid will be easy to provoke into a fight, but Travers will take a lot of pushing, but there's a way . . . Sophie Coleman. Threaten her and you'll soon have Travers on your tail. With the kid and Travers out of the way, there'll be no stopping me. I'll own this whole valley.'

Fallon still had doubts. Lonegan was making it sound too easy, almost as if he was afraid of something and afraid to admit it, even to himself.

'Anyone else we should worry about?' he asked softly.

'Just one,' Stroud said suddenly, cursing silently as he became aware of Lonegan's angry glance at him. It would take him a long time to get back into Lonegan's good books again if he ever made it that far.

'Who?' Towney snapped, his interest suddenly aroused.

Stroud shrugged. Hiding from the truth wouldn't make it go away. It was best out in the open. Anyway the damage was already done, and there was no going back on it now.

'John Cord,' he answered quietly.

Again Fallon searched his memory. John Cord. The name meant nothing to him, and he knew every fast gun around, had to. It was a matter of survival.

'Describe him!' The words came out flat and cold. The man named Cord had clearly impressed Stroud, and had to be considered dangerous, until proved otherwise.

'Tall, lean, walks and talks soft. Doesn't say much but can handle himself with his fists. Pretty good with a rifle, too.'

'How does he carry his gun? Cross draw, left hand, butt forward?'

'As far as I know, he doesn't carry a side gun, only a rifle.'

Fallon looked at Lonegan, trying to make sense of his information. For some reason Stroud seemed afraid of Cord, but why? Hell, the man didn't even carry a pistol.

'He's nothing,' Lonegan said flatly. 'He's just a saddletramp. At the first sign of trouble he'll ride away.'

Somehow the words didn't ring true. Lonegan, too, had doubts about John Cord, and that was cause for thought. Whoever John Cord was, he meant trouble. Well, with a little luck Caleb Towney would run into him first.

23

Sophie Coleman came to an abrupt halt as she came around the corner of her house and found herself facing four riders. Once again she had been caught flat-footed, her old rifle still inside the house. Since Cord had run off her last visitors, she had expected no further trouble, but should have known better.

Three of the men she knew, but the fourth was a stranger. One of Lonegan's new hired guns? He had that look about him.

Fallon swore silently. Threatening women went against the grain, but it was better that he took this job than Laine or Towney. There was no telling what would happen if they were here.

At least, the most that Sophie Coleman would lose today was her home. With Towney . . . He left the thought unfinished.

'What do you want?' Sophie asked, her stance proud and defiant.

She had guts, Fallon decided, and if she had a rifle to hand there would have been hell to pay. Still, there was a job to be done, and if he failed Lonegan would send Towney to finish the job. He didn't like that idea. At least with him, Sophie Coleman would go on living.

'Lonegan wants this place wiped out, ma'am,' he said softly. 'It ain't to my liking either, but it's got to be done. If there's anything special you want from the house it's best that you get it now before we set the place on fire. One of my men will go with you, just so you don't do nothing foolish.' He paused. 'I'm sorry it's got to be this way, ma'am.'

'Not as sorry as you are going to be if you don't ride out now, Fallon,' Cord said, stepping out from the shelter of the barn, his rifle ready and pointing at Jim Fallon.

Fallon shook his head slowly. 'Knew

this job wasn't going to be as easy as Lonegan figured it would be. Guess he just didn't know what he was up against. If I had known . . . '

'If you had known you wouldn't be here threatening women. Is that it, Fallon?'

'It was either me, Laine or Towney. I volunteered because I didn't like the idea of Laine or Towney coming here. You the one they call Cord?'

'That's what they call me,' Cord said softly.

'That figures. Stroud was right about you, but he didn't know how right he was. But nobody was listening to him. He tried to warn us about you, but I wasn't listening either.'

'You listening now, Fallon?' Cord asked softly.

'I'm listening, Cord. I've never been dumb enough to go up against you before. I'm not about to make that mistake now. If I got the chance, I'd head right back where I came from. Have I got that chance, Cord?'

'You got that chance, Fallon,' Cord said quietly. 'You going to tell Laine and Towney about me before you leave?'

Fallon grinned. 'Hell, no. Let them make their own mistakes.' He paused. 'Don't take no chances with Towney, Cord. He's as quick as a rattler and twice as mean. Shoot him in the back if you get the chance. Nobody will ever blame you for it.'

He reined his roan around slowly, confident that Cord wouldn't shoot him, unless he started something. There was no way he was about to do that . . . only a fool took chances with a man like John Cord.

Glancing at the other three men, he said softly, 'If any of you are thinking of starting anything, forget it. Remember you will have two guns against you, Cord's and mine.'

There was no mistaking the threat in his words. Any man who started anything now would die.

Lonegan glared at his three men. 'I sent four men out to scare away one lone woman, and you fail. What happened?'

'John Cord was there,' Kilby said quietly.

'He's still only one man, Kilby,' Lonegan snapped. 'I hired Jim Fallon to take care of the likes of Cord. Where is he?'

'Out in the bunkhouse, packing up to move on. I had the feeling that he knew John Cord, and didn't like what he was up against. If I didn't know better, I'd say he was scared.'

He stopped talking as Fallon entered, carrying his bedroll. 'I've come to collect my money, Lonegan,' he said softly. He had heard Kilby but hadn't taken offence. Hell, it was the truth, anyway.

'You taking money for running away, Fallon?' Lonegan asked.

'Sure. That way I get to spend it,' Fallon said easily.

'You letting one man run you out?' Towney asked. 'You're yeller, Fallon.'

'I'm still living, Towney. If I had tried anything today I wouldn't be. I like living. About that money, Lonegan . . . '

Still angry, Lonegan reached into his billfold. Fallon was running out on him, and he didn't like that. No man had ever run out on him before, and no one would ever run out on him again. He would make sure of that.

His eyes met Towney's and he nodded. The whitehaired man knew what that meant. He would take care of Fallon, but not here, not now.

The money disappeared into Fallon's shirt pocket and he started to back out slowly.

He felt no regrets about taking Lonegan's money. Hell, the big man wouldn't need money where he was heading. Too bad he couldn't stay around long enough to see it, but he had given Cord his word.

He would have given a lot to be here when Cord finally cut loose.

24

'Fallon's dead,' Jonas said flatly as he dismounted slowly from his borrowed horse. He was only vaguely aware of the others on the porch as he faced John Cord.

Strange, there was no sign of relief on the tall man's face, only regret. That didn't make sense. Cord should be happy that the odds had been shortened in his favour.

'What happened?' Cord asked flatly.

Jonas shrugged. 'No one knows for sure. They found his body on the trail — shot in the back. Lonegan claims that one of the Triangle boys did it, under orders from Travers. The funny thing is Fallon had his bedroll tied behind his saddle as if he was riding out.'

'He was,' Cord said softly. Fallon was too good a man to die that way. Sure, he made his living with a gun, but so did a lot of men, and Fallon always drew a line between what he would and wouldn't do.

The killing had all the hallmarks of Caleb Towney and, no doubt, under orders from Jud Lonegan.

He looked at Jonas again. The man had more to say but was reluctant to say it, glancing nervously at Jane and Brad. Whatever he had to say concerned them, but he didn't want to say it in front of them.

'Want to take a ride, Jonas?' Cord asked quietly.

The old man nodded, watching Cord move towards the big Appaloosa. He was aware of Travers moving towards them. 'Need company?'

'Might be best,' Jonas agreed. It was better that the news be kept from Jane and Brad, and they could depend upon Travers to keep his mouth shut.

They rode slowly, Cord holding Warrior back to keep pace with the other horses. The big horse liked a fast pace, and didn't like being restrained. After a while they reined in near a small creek.

'Get it said, Jonas,' Travers said abruptly as he dismounted to let his horse drink. There was no use in hiding from bad news.

'Lonegan's put a price on your heads . . . you and Brad's. He wants you both dead. With Brad dead, he figures that will take the fight out of the other ranchers.'

'He's got no reason for killing us,' Travers said. If there was any way to avoid a fight he would find it.

'Morey Laine wants you dead because he reckons you killed Fallon, or gave the orders. Towney wants Brad dead because he claims that Taco was a friend of his. The next time you ride into town you'll find either Laine or Towney waiting for you . . . maybe both. Leaving your gun behind won't work any more. They'll find a gun on your body after you are dead. Anyway, there will be no witnesses around to say how you died.'

'He's running a bluff,' Travers said quietly. 'Lonegan doesn't want a shooting war any more than we do.'

'Nobody hires the likes of Caleb Towney on a bluff,' Jonas said sharply. 'You know, for a smart man, Travers, you ain't very bright. You know Towney's reputation.'

'Men like Towney blow up their own reputations to scare people. It makes life easier for them. When the chips are down, they're no different to anyone else.'

Cord finished rolling his cigarette and lit it, shaking his head slowly. Travers was even lying to himself now.

'You think Lonegan is afraid of killing, Travers?' he asked softly.

'He hasn't done any yet,' Travers pointed out. 'There's no real reason for him to start anything now. All he wants to do is frighten everyone away from the valley. That's the reason he hired Towney.'

'That's just part of it, Travers,' Cord said quietly. 'You know Towney's history?'

'I heard rumours, Cord. Something about him starting his killing career with Bloody Bill Anderson during the war. There was no controlling him then and there is no controlling him now. They say he's only ever taken orders from one man in his life. What kind of man could give Towney orders and make him like it, Cord?'

'The worst kind,' Cord answered quietly. 'And he's still giving his orders. All he needed was a change of name. There are still a lot of men out there looking for Captain Elim Trask.'

The full intent of Cord's words hit Travers hard. 'Lonegan? You think that Jud Lonegan is Elim Trask?' He shook his head, 'It can't be. Some say he was as evil as Towney, in some ways worse. If you are right, no one in this valley is safe. Men like Trask don't change. If . . . Jane, Debbie, no one's safe.'

'It's your job to make sure that they stay safe, Trav. I want you to keep every man close to the ranch, armed and

217

ready to kill, until this is all over.'

'What are you going to do, Cord?'

'If my guess is right, Lonegan will be keeping Towney close to his side as insurance. Morey Laine will be in town with a couple of men in case you or Brad ride in.'

'That still doesn't answer my question, Cord,' Travers said.

'I'm going to find out if Morey Laine is as big as his reputation,' Cord answered softly.

A chill went through Jonas's bones. He had always known that the tall man was dangerous, but this time Lonegan had pushed Cord to the limit. The tall man was going hunting and God help Lonegan.

Jonas had never seen Cord use a gun, but he had the feeling that it was second nature to the man. He would know for sure when Cord rode into town tonight. It would be tonight. That much he was sure of. Cord had already put off the showdown for too long. There was regret in the tall man that it had come to this, but he was ready to face it without fear.

* * *

The sun was setting, but Jane was hardly aware of it. The washing up had been completed. The evening was her own, yet she felt the need to share it with someone. Anyone. She had a bad feeling creeping up on her that she didn't like. Travers had disappeared with Brad soon after eating. John Cord had disappeared too. The men had something in mind. For some reason it seemed that both men had wanted Brad out of the way but she didn't know why, until now.

She felt sick as she spotted that big Colt hanging on his right hip. The weapon had become a part of the man again. He stopped before her, his face gentle.

'There's no need for this, Johnny,' she pleaded. 'Please don't go. Please.'

'If I don't go to them, Jane, they'll

come to us. Even a stray bullet can kill. I can't take a chance on you or Debbie getting hurt that way.'

'Will . . . will you be coming back?'

'If I can, but I won't be stopping, Jane.'

'We need you here, Johnny, and you won't be needing a gun ever again. Please.'

He avoided her lovely eyes; knowing he couldn't look into those depths and refuse her anything.

'There is no future here for us, Jane. Never has been and never will be, but I'll never forget you or Debbie. You'll be a part of me for the rest of my life . . . the best part.'

He mounted quickly, knowing he could never find all the words he needed to tell her how he felt about her. It would take a lifetime to do that.

He rode out of the yard without looking back. Leaving the valley would be the hardest decision he would ever have to make, but he had no choice.

Perhaps it would be best if he left the valley straight after settling with Lonegan . . . if he could. Caleb Towney and Morey Laine would have other plans for him.

The vision of her misty-eyed loveliness stayed with him — would stay with him forever — as he rode towards town.

The dream had died inside him but the vision would remain. Travers had been right; there was no future here for him, never could be.

Soon . . . too soon, there would be another would-be gunslinger on his trail, a hot-headed kid with a fast gun, and an urge to kill the man who had killed his father.

There would be no winners in that fight.

25

Morey Laine looked up quickly as the tall man entered the saloon, rain dripping from his widebrimmed JB. It wasn't the man who interested Laine, just that big black Colt hanging on the man's hip like it belonged there.

'Who is he?' he whispered from the corner of his mouth.

'John Cord,' Kilby said quietly, but this was a different John Cord from the man he had seen around. This man had a cold deadly look about him that made Kilby shiver.

He had never seen Cord wearing a gun before, but there was no doubt that he could use that lethal-looking weapon.

Morey Laine was in trouble. Lonegan, too. Kilby shrugged. It didn't look as if he would get his wages this month. He got to his feet suddenly, moving away from Morey Laine. With his thumb and forefinger he plucked his gun from the holster and laid it on the bar, stepping away quickly.

He had no intention of getting shot, even by accident. That still left two men against Cord, if Skip was dumb enough to back Morey. He glanced at Skip. Yeah, he was dumb enough.

'You're Morey Laine?' Cord asked quietly. 'I hear you've been waiting for Col Travers.'

'I'm still waiting, Cord. Got a message from him?'

'Yeah. He isn't coming. I told him not to. I wanted to keep the pleasure of killing you for myself.'

Laine got to his feet slowly. The man was too confident. But he had no reputation to back it up. He felt Skip rising from his chair at his side, ready to back him up. He was a pretty good gun, and could prove useful.

Almost without thought, he felt his hand dip, as smooth a draw as he had ever made. He felt sudden panic as he saw Cord's gun sweep up, and felt the heavy slug drive him back towards the wall. There was no second shot. No need. Cord had known exactly where his bullet was going.

Morey was dead before his back hit the wall.

Skip had barely touched his gunbutt before he found himself covered by Cord's gun. He could hardly breathe as he looked into the muzzle of that big black Colt. He was about to die and there was nothing he could do about it.

He was feeling now the way Bearcat Riley must have felt when he faced Cord for the second time, but at least Riley was still living. There was little chance of that for him.

'You've got a chance to go on living, mister,' Cord said. 'Do you want that chance?'

Skip nodded, unable to speak for the moment.

'Good. You can ride out to Lonegan's place, tell Towney and Elim Trask that I'll be waiting right here for them.'

'Trask? There's nobody called Trask working for Lonegan.'

'Just pass on the message. They'll come.'

Skip and Kilby had both disappeared, along with Morey's body, as Jonas sidled up to the bar. John Cord sat in the corner, his face thoughtful. He had been forced to kill again, and didn't like it . . . had never liked it.

But there was more to come.

Jonas lifted a bottle and two glasses from the bar, for the first time without protest from the bartender, and carried them towards John Cord. Maybe a drink would ease the tall man's suffering. At least, it would help.

Elim Trask. That was the name of Caleb Towney's captain during the war. When he heard that name, Lonegan would come. Had to, if he wanted to go on living. If it was known that Elim Trask was still around, there would be a hundred men riding into the valley looking to hang him . . . or worse.

Yeah, he would come. He had no choice.

Jonas poured a drink, pushing it towards Cord, and was surprised to see the tall man drain it in one go. The tall man needed a hard drink this time. But only one. His hand covered the glass when Jonas tried to pour a second.

Killing had never come easy to Cord, and never would. Soon, he would have to kill again, or be killed. But the killing of Towney and Trask wouldn't cause him any pain. It was just something that had to be done. Later . . .

He didn't like to think of what was to follow. Maybe it would be best if he died right here along with Towney and Trask.

Jonas, sensing that Cord needed to be alone, got to his feet, reluctantly leaving the bottle behind as he moved out on to the porch. Out there he could do some good by warning Cord of Towney and Trask's arrival.

The rain was dying out now, leaving a chill in the air as Jonas settled himself in his chair, his eyes intent on the south side of the street, the direction that Towney and Trask would come from.

They would come alone, Jonas was sure of that. Lonegan wouldn't want any of his men to hear the name of Elim Trask spoken. There were still a lot of men around with long memories. Maybe with the killing of John Cord he could also kill the memory of Elim Trask.

Cord waited, his mind blank, not allowing himself to think of anything. A split-second distraction when it came to the showdown could result in his death and he didn't want to die until he saw Towney and Trask breathe their last.

They were coming. Cord got to his feet slowly as Jonas came through the doors, and nodded. 'The two of them,' he said quietly as he passed Cord and moved to the far corner of the room.

There was no way he was going to miss this. He had been waiting a long time to see Lonegan get his — a lot of people had. The thought that Cord might lose never occurred to him. Even if they did kill Cord, it was a sure bet that the tall man would take them both with him.

The tall man was ready, as ready as he would ever be. Ready to kill or ready to die.

Towney was first through the doors, stepping quickly aside for Jud Lonegan to enter. Those pale eyes sought out Cord, recognizing him for what he was. For the first time in his life, Towney felt doubts. There was an easy confidence about the man that he found disturbing. Hell, his reputation was enough to scare most men half to death. Facing him started men trembling with fear. But not John Cord. For the first time, he was facing a man without doubts or fears. And that bothered him.

Still he would teach John Cord fear before he died.

The fact that the man had no reputation still bothered him. John

Cord? The name meant nothing to him. The tall man was running a bluff, and Towney was about to call it.

'You're John Cord?' he asked quietly.

'That's what they call me,' Cord answered softly. 'And you are Caleb Towney.'

'The name mean anything to you, Cord?'

'About as much as it does to everyone else, Towney. I'm a little disappointed in you. A man with a reputation like yours shouldn't need to shoot someone like Jim Fallon in the back. He was too good a man to die that way.'

Towney's normally pale face blanched even more. Cord's guess had hit the mark, but that fact didn't bother him. He couldn't prove anything. But the man was pushing him, goading him, and he didn't like that. No one had ever pushed him like that before.

'You talk too much, Cord,' he said angrily.

Cord glanced at Lonegan. So far the

big man hadn't spoken. He was waiting for Towney to push Cord into a gunfight before joining in. He would let his gun do the talking. Rumour had it that he was almost as good with a gun as Towney.

Things weren't turning out the way they planned. Cord was doing the pushing, taking the play away from them.

'It's a failing of mine,' Cord admitted. 'It gives me something to do while I'm waiting for you to find guts enough to pull that gun of yours. Would it help if I turned my back?'

That was the final straw. Towney's hand swept down to his gun, but too late. Cord's gun was already rising and spitting death. His first bullet slammed deep into Towney's chest, driving the breath from his body. Cord's second bullet killed Lonegan where he stood, his gun sliding back into leather as he died.

He had been warned, but wouldn't listen. It was too late now.

Cord stepped over to Towney, watching the life ebb from the man's body. It was never pleasant to watch a man die — even a man like Towney.

'I know you now,' Towney said quietly. 'They were right. You are the best. If I had known . . . if . . . '

He died quietly, torn between hate and admiration for the man who had killed him.

26

She waited, her face pale and her breathing shallow as she searched the darkness, and listened for the sounds of hoofbeats. He had been gone a long time, too long. Perhaps he had changed his mind and left the valley without coming back here.

No, Cord wouldn't do that. He had said he would be back, and John Cord always kept his word. He would be back, but he wouldn't be staying. That was one fact that she would have to accept, even though it hurt so much. Life at the Triangle wouldn't be the same after he left, for her or Debbie. The fact that they would never see him again after tonight filled her with fear. It would destroy Debbie, too.

She glanced at Travers and the other Triangle men. Like her, they all knew of Cord's visit to town and his reason for going there. Even Brad looked worried.

Finally, the big Appaloosa hove into view, and they all breathed a sigh of relief. John Cord was back and he was unhurt. He dismounted in front of Jane, letting the reins dangle over the hitching rail.

'It's over,' he said quietly. 'I'll be taking the last gun out of the valley with me.'

'Please, Johnny, please.'

'It's for the best, Jane. We both know that. We would both be living a lie. Sooner or later, that lie would catch up with us and destroy us both. Debbie, too. I can't live with that.'

He moved back towards Warrior and gathered up the reins. There was no sense in prolonging the agony. It was best that he ride away now before the truth caught up with him.

'Bodell!'

The name stopped him in his tracks. He let the reins fall and stepped away from Warrior. In the event of gunplay, he didn't want the big horse hurt.

Reluctantly, he faced Brad. He had hoped that this day would never come, but deep inside had known that there was no way to avoid it. A man could never really hide from his past.

Three men had already died beneath his gun tonight. The thought that Brad would be the fourth sickened him but there was nothing he could do about it. He had already warned Brad what would happen when he faced up to a real gunfighter.

He had been using a gun for too long. When Brad went for his gun he would die. He would kill Brad. He would have no choice. His gunfighter's instinct would take over and Brad would die. There would be no time for thought, there never was.

Whatever feelings Jane and Debbie had for him would die along with Brad. He would die inside, too.

'I knew we would meet up one day, Bodell. I've been waiting a long time for this. You killed my father and now I'm going to kill you.'

'Sorry, Cord,' Brazos said quietly. 'I've got a big mouth, but I didn't know about the kid's father.'

'It had to come out sooner or later,' Cord said softly. 'I didn't know either until a few days ago.'

'You're faster than me, Cord,' Brad snarled, 'But there's not enough bullets in that gun of yours to stop me killing you.'

'Don't try it, boy. You don't have a chance and I don't want to kill you. I'm riding out. Don't try to stop me.'

He glanced at Jane's ashen face, and knew only one man would die in this yard tonight. And it wouldn't be Brad. He couldn't hurt Jane again.

'On the count of three, Bodell,' Brad said. 'One. Two. Three.'

His hand swept down, his gun rising and spitting flame before he was aware of the fact that Cord's gun was in his hand and had been for some time.

Brad's bullet slammed into Cord driving him back into the hitching rail. Strangely, there was no pain yet, only a numbness. He watched Brad advance, his gun cocked again and ready.

'I'm going to finish the job now, Cord.'

'Want to bet that I can kill you before you kill Cord, Brad?' Col Travers yelled. 'Remember, you already lost one bet to me.'

The cocking of his pistol accompanied his words.

Brad kept his eye on Cord. The tall man still had his hand on his gun and he was far more dangerous than Travers. Travers wouldn't shoot him. He had known him too long.'

'You're bluffing, Col.'

'Am I, Brad? Cord won't kill you but I will, and I won't regret it. I'm the man you really want. I'm the man most responsible for your father's death.'

A sudden silence greeted his words. 'Sorry Jane, but I've been living a lie, too. That's part of the reason I wanted Cord away from this valley. I told you I was with Tom the night he died, but I didn't tell you everything. As usual,

Tom had been drinking. You know how he got when he had been drinking and gambling. Most of the money we got from the cattle sale vanished across a poker table. It seemed like an easy way for Tom to recoup his losses when he spotted Jack Bodell. He had a price of five thousand dollars on his head then, a case of mistaken identity as it turned out later. To Tom it seemed like easy money and he didn't care how he got it.

'He was sneaking up on Bodell with a shotgun when I yelled to warn him. I don't like back-shooters. Tom died because he didn't have the guts to face up to any man. Bodell killed him because he had no choice. I'd do the same thing again. Why don't you shoot him in the back, Brad, finish the job the way your father tried to do it?

'Brazos!' his voice snapped out again, but his eye never left Brad. If the kid tried anything now, he would kill him. 'Ride into town. Get the doc out here and make it fast.'

Brazos was already halfway to the

stables before the words had left Travers' mouth. It was his damned fault that Cord was lying there with a bullet in him, anyway. It was a poor excuse that he hadn't known about Brad's father. If he had known that it was going to turn out like this he would have shot Brad himself.

'You're a liar, Travers. My father would never do anything like that.'

'How would you know, Brad? He was never around this place long enough for you to get to know him. Both your mother and me know different. I knew your father for the best part of thirty years, and I knew his shortcomings. You knew him for ten years, Brad. How much time did he spend with you? How much love did he ever show you? It would have been the same with Debbie, had he been around. In a few weeks Cord has shown Jane and Debbie more love and consideration than Tom would have ever done, even if he had lived to be a hundred. You, too, but you are too much of a fool to realize it.'

'You're still a liar, Travers,' Brad said, advancing on Cord.

'One more step and you are dead, Brad,' Travers snapped.

'Everything he's said is true,' Jane said, moving off the porch to kneel beside John Cord. She couldn't think of him as Jack Bodell. Jack Bodell was dead. John Cord had killed him.

The wound didn't look too serious. At least, she hoped not. John Cord was a strong man, able to withstand a lot of pain. She looked towards her men for aid in moving Cord into the house, but Brad was still between her and them, and the gun was still in Brad's hand.

'Everyone warned me against marrying Tom, but I didn't want to hear them. I knew better, but I was lying to myself. He reminded me of someone I had met briefly, but thought I would never see again. I know now it was nothing more than a slight physical resemblance. Tom could never even hope to live in that man's shadow. Jack Bodell is dead, Brad. He's been dead for a long time. It was a man called John Cord who rode into town tonight to face three killers alone. They weren't expecting him, but he is the only man here who could have gone into town and come out alive again. Morey Laine was waiting for you, Brad. He would have killed you without a second thought, but he faced a man called John Cord instead. That's the reason — the only reason — you are still living. You really think you beat him to the draw tonight, Brad? You didn't. Cord could have killed you three times before you cleared leather. He could have killed you, but he didn't. Doesn't that tell you anything about John Cord? How many lives have you got? Can you afford to throw them away so easily?'

'We both know why he didn't kill me: it was because of you and Debbie. Hell, if I had braced him alone, it would have been different.'

'Would it, Brad?' she asked softly. 'Doesn't the fact that John Cord took your place tonight tell you anything? He could have let Morey Laine kill you tonight, and that would have been an end to all his problems. Debbie and I couldn't have blamed him for that, could we?'

'I still think . . . '

'No, boy,' Travers snapped. 'You ain't thinking at all. Fact is, I'm starting to believe you ain't capable of thinking. Hell, Cord has no real reason for liking you, other than you are Jane's son and Debbie's brother. Truth is, I don't know of anyone who has any real liking for you. I had hopes for you once, but . . . You got a lot of growing up to do, boy, but I wonder if you are going to have time enough to do it.'

He watched the gun start to sag in Brad's hand. Either the kid didn't like the odds or he was starting to see sense. Still, Travers wouldn't be taking any chances with him.

'The doc will be out soon, Cord. He'll take care of you. I'll be keeping an eye on Brad for as long as you are here. When you are ready you can ride out,

Brad won't be stopping you.'

He watched Brad slide his gun back into leather before stepping forward to stand over Cord.

'Why didn't you kill me when you had the chance, Cord?'

'I figured I'd already taken enough off you and your family, Brad,' Cord answered quietly.

'Don't even think about trying to stop him riding out, Brad,' said Col Travers. 'As long as Cord is here, I'm not letting you out of my sight.'

'Cord isn't going anywhere, Travers,' Brad said quietly. 'I am. You were right about me, Travers, I have got a lot of growing up to do, but I can't do it here. I need space, plenty of time to think, and try to unscramble my brain. Here, I'm the boss's son. I don't take orders: I give them. Out there I'm nobody. I'll have to make my own way. There's a lot of country I haven't seen, a lot of trail drives I haven't been on. I think a man can grow better, think more clearly in open country. There is one last order

I'd like to give, Travers. I'd like someone to saddle my horse for me and fill my saddlebags with grub. I got a long ride ahead of me.'

He paused, looking down at Cord. 'You've made leaving easy for me, Cord. I've had a hankering to see some new country for a long time, but I guess I was afraid of leaving Ma and Debbie. I can ease my mind now, knowing that they will be taken care of better than I ever could.'

He paused, tapping his gunbutt. 'Don't worry about this thing, Cord. I've done all the practising I'm ever going to do. I still get a sick feeling in my stomach when I think of Taco. I hope I never forget that feeling. I've learned a lot from you, Cord. It took a long time, but I've learned. I hope I will have learned a lot more by the next time we meet. I got no need to tell you to take care of Ma and Debbie for me until then, have I?'

Mention of Debbie made Cord wonder where she was. Jane touched him gently, reading his mind. 'She's inside with Sophie, Johnny. She called when you were in town to see Travers. Lem Neelson is looking after her place until she gets back. You'll see Debbie after we get you patched up.'

He nodded, relieved, before turning his attention back to Brad.

'Your place is here with your family, Brad,' he said flatly.

'I'll be back when I've grown up, Cord. I've got my own life to live for now. I hope I've made all the mistakes I'm going to make, but I doubt it.'

He glanced around as Chick led his horse from the stables. 'I'm glad I'm not as good a shot as I thought I was.'

'You pulled it, Brad,' Cord said. 'When the chips were down you didn't really want to kill me.'

'I think you mean that. Thanks. You belong here, Cord. It took you a long time to get here, but this is your place. Your life can begin right here. I hope you are man enough to do something about it.'

He reached for his horse's reins, swinging easily into the saddle, before looking down at Cord again, and grinning suddenly. 'Just one more thing — when I get back I'll expect to hear Debbie calling you Pa, or you'll have real trouble on your hands.'

THE END

Other titles in the
Linford Western Library:

DEAD IS FOR EVER

Amy Sadler

After rescuing Hope Bennett from the clutches of two trailbums, Sam Carver made a serious mistake. He killed one of the outlaws, and reckoned on collecting the bounty on Lew Daggett. But catching Sam off-guard, Daggett made off with the girl, leaving Sam for dead. However, he was only grazed and once he came to, he set out in search of Hope. When he eventually found her, he was forced into a dramatic showdown with his life on the line.

SMOKING STAR

B. J. Holmes

In the one-horse town of Medicine Bluff two men were dead. Sheriff Jack Starr didn't need the badge on his chest to spur him into tracking the killer. He had his own reason for seeking justice, a reason no-one knew. It drove him to take a journey into the past where he was to discover something else that was to add even greater urgency to the situation — to stop Montana's rivers running red with blood.